Copyright © Alberto Rivera 2024. All rights reserved.
No part of this book may be reproduced, distributed, or transmitted in any form or by any means, including photocopying, recording, or other electronic or mechanical methods, without the prior written permission of the publisher, except in the case of brief quotations embodied in critical reviews and certain other noncommercial uses permitted by copyright law.

This is a work of fiction. Names, characters, places, and incidents either are the product of the author's imagination or are used fictitiously. Any resemblance to actual persons, living or dead, or actual events is purely coincidental.

DEDICATION

To my family, whose never-ending unconditional love and
encouragement have been the light of every step of this journey.
You are my inspiration and my joy.
This debut book is dedicated to you.

CONTENTS

	Acknowledgments
1	Harper's Tragedy
2	Awakening
3	Detective Andrews
4	Concussion Protocol
5	An Eclipse Tattoo
6	The Wake & a gun
7	A Funeral and an Epiphany
8	Information Gathering
9	Hector Cartwright
10	Cartwright's Fate
11	Industrial District's Massacre
12	Detective Andrews
13	Carlos Delgado
14	Anguish: Past and Present
15	Unlikely Alliances
16	The Setup
17	Isabella Vargas
18	Giving In

ACKNOWLEDGMENTS

In heartfelt appreciation to my family: Karen, whose support
and encouragement fueled my late-night writing sessions;
Alberto Jr., whose lively spirit and games
kept me grounded throughout;
and Aliana, whose award-winning poem at a
writing fair sparked my creative journey
and inspired me to pen this tale.

Grateful acknowledgment to my family and friends
for believing in me.

Special thanks to James Thayer, whose insightful Spotify podcast
episodes provided me invaluable guidance in
sharpening my writing toolkit.

To all who believed in me along this journey,
your encouragement made this story possible.
Thank you, and I hope you enjoy
this thrilling narrative:
The Man of Foundry Hills.

Chapter 1: Harper's Tragedy

In the throbbing heart of Foundry Hills, corruption and deceit held sway. Skyscrapers soared, clawing at the sky, each locked in a silent battle for dominance within the concrete jungle. Pedestrians rushed along, their faces set with purpose yet void of emotion, reflecting the chaotic rhythms of the traffic swirling around them. Here, it seemed humanity had bartered away its soul for just a glimpse of success.

To the northwest of this relentless urban sprawl, Warren Court rested under a canopy of dark, brooding clouds. In this enclave, houses stood apart in serene isolation, their tranquil existence a stark contrast to the rampant crime that infected the city. One home, brimming with the memories of a reclusive family, shone as a tranquil beacon amidst the surrounding turmoil.

James Harper, with deliberate movements, retrieved his glasses from the sink counter. He meticulously wiped the lenses clean, restoring the world to clarity for his piercing blue eyes. Outside, rain hammered against the windows, its drumming a backdrop to the muffled voices that seeped in from the hallway.

Suddenly, the house plunged into a moment of stark darkness before the lights stuttered back to life. Harper's gaze snapped upwards at the intermittent outage.

From the kitchen, Denise's voice cut through the quiet, "Harp?"

"It's just a brownout," Harper called back, his tone reassuring. "I'll be out in a second."

He reached into his hoodie pocket, fingers brushing against the elegantly wrapped box labeled "For my love." A smile played on his lips as he envisioned the gold necklace and emerald pendant inside, picturing Denise's delight upon seeing it. The emerald's luster brought back memories of their first meeting—her eyes had sparkled just as brightly. Now, over a decade later, the pendant seemed the perfect embodiment of their enduring connection. With a sense of relish for the moment yet to come, he tucked the box away again.

As he strode down the hallway, lightning flared, casting stark light on the family photos that lined the walls. He paused to peer through the drapes, watching as the relentless rain swelled a nearby creek, the waters surging over its banks, unable to contain the wild deluge.

Harper joined his children in the living room, where the laughter of Alice and James Jr. enveloped the space with warmth as they tossed dice across their board game. In the kitchen, Denise stirred a pot, then sealed it with a lid. The tantalizing aroma of beef stew—rich with vegetables and herbs—wafted through the air, filling the house with its hearty scent.

Denise walked into the living room, a bowl of popcorn in hand. "I know that look," she said, eyeing him playfully.

"What look? This is just my normal face," Harper replied with a grin, his eyes briefly flitting from the laptop perched on his lap.

Her smile broadened as she settled next to him on the couch. The melancholic strains of Beethoven's "Moonlight Sonata" emanated softly from the radio, setting a serene backdrop. Harper inhaled deeply, savoring the aroma of the stew. "You know, without your amazing cooking, I'd be surviving on microwave meals and instant noodles," he joked. "I don't know what I'd do without you."

Denise's gaze softened as she placed the bowl down and gently touched his hand. "You'd be living on bland food, missing all the flavor I bring to your life," she teased, her smile playful. "I love you, Harp."

"I love you too, Deni," he replied. Their eyes drifted to a photo above the fireplace, capturing the four of them posing in front of red peonies at Rolling Peaks.

Denise rested her head on Harper's chest, her presence a comforting weight. Harper breathed in deeply, the scent of her long red hair filling his senses. Below them, Alice and James Jr. continued their game, their laughter a gentle soundtrack to the evening.

The room's shadows danced to the flickering flames in the fireplace. Suddenly, the peaceful scene shattered with the sound of glass breaking at the front door. Harper's heart lurched as he locked eyes with Denise in alarm.

Through the mirror above the fireplace, Harper caught sight of three masked, armed gunmen storming in. Their menacing demeanor left no doubt about their intentions. Harper's protective instincts surged; he stood to confront the threat, but a savage blow to his head sent him reeling to his knees, pain radiating through his skull. Denise's scream sliced through the chaos as she witnessed blood trickle down his neck.

With a desperate effort, Harper grabbed the laptop from the coffee table and hurled it at one of the intruders, striking them squarely and knocking them unconscious.

As Harper struggled to his feet, another intruder grabbed Denise, pressing a gun to her head. The assailant's hand, marked with a circular tattoo, was stark against her skin. Harper raised his hands, his voice strained with urgency. "Please, take anything you want. Just let her go."

A second assailant approached, his chuckle dark and menacing as he drew nearer to Harper.

"Let's not keep the Sandman waiting," the assailant taunted in a thick Hispanic accent, his words dripping with malice. He delivered a swift, powerful blow to Harper's head, and Harper crumpled to the floor, unconscious.

Gunshots erupted, lighting up the room as their deafening roar merged with the storm's fury battering Warren Court. The barrage of bullets was relentless, echoing the chaos of the tempest outside.

When the gunsmoke cleared, an eerie silence descended upon the house. The only sound was the bubbling of the stew left simmering on the stove, its rich aroma a stark contrast to the violence that had just torn through the home. Outside, the storm continued unabated, its raging winds mirroring the chaos that had unfolded within.

Chapter 2: Awakening

Harper awoke to an intense headache, his senses gradually tuning into the grim reality as he lay on the floor. The distant sound of car doors slamming shut and a vehicle racing away echoed through the quiet cul-de-sac. Beside him, the carpet was soaked with a pool of blood, and the sharp scent of smoke mingled with blood filled the air. Turning his head, he found Denise motionless beside him. "Denise, I can't move... my head... it hurts," he rasped, his voice choked with pain. The silence that followed sent shivers down his spine.

"Denise...?" he called again, desperation edging into his voice.

Slowly, he reached out, his hand shaking as he touched her shoulder. Her body shifted limply, her eyes, once lively and vibrant, now unsettlingly still. Clasping her lifeless form, Harper's breath hitched, a wave of disbelief washing over him. "No, God no, this can't be happening," he whispered, his voice breaking as his world seemed to shatter around him.

The harsh reality of his situation settled in; his worst fears had materialized. The intruders had vanished, leaving behind only devastation. He clasped Denise's hand—still warm, heartbreakingly deceptive as if life lingered there. His mind was flooded with intense memories of their life together; her bright, loving eyes had always been his anchor in any storm. He could nearly hear the sound of her laughter at his jokes, a comforting presence that once filled their home. Now, gripping her hand, Harper was submerged in an ocean of grief, the weight of his loss crushing him. The vibrant woman he had vowed to spend his life with now felt impossibly distant.

On his knees, he gently cradled Denise's head against his chest, tears quietly tracing down his face as he kissed her forehead softly. With a final loving touch, he closed her emerald-green eyes, a tender farewell to the love of his life. Whispering a final, heart-wrenching goodbye, he gently laid her down. Then, with a resolve born of necessity, he turned to find his children, Alice and James, his heart heavy with dread.

"Alice? James?" Harper's voice was thick with emotion as he called out into the eerie silence of the house. No answer came, only the sound of his heartbeat thundering in his ears. Panic surged within him as he scanned the living room, finding no trace of his children. With a body aching from earlier blows, he forced himself to his feet, driven by a desperate need to find them. Popcorn and blood littered the floor, a dark testament to the night's violence. Stumbling out of the living room, the crunch of popcorn underfoot sounded like brittle autumn leaves. Harper prayed fervently for his children's safety.

"James? Alice?" His voice quivered with each call, steps faltering as his head throbbed from the earlier blows.

He passed by the children's bathroom—no sign of them. Faint sounds from James' room quickened his pulse. Heart pounding, he pushed the door open and called out, "James?" The television played one of James Jr.'s favorite cartoons, triggering memories of Denise gently reminding him to turn it off. Searching under the bed, he found only empty snack wrappers. Exiting the room, he noticed Alice's door was ajar.

"Alice... James..." His voice was desperate as he entered, his eyes scanning every corner, but the room was empty.

Something in his peripheral vision caught his attention towards the open closet. His eyes shifted towards it.

"Alice?"

His peripheral vision caught a movement near the open closet. "Alice?" Hope flickered briefly as he approached, praying they might be hiding safely inside. But as he opened the door wider, his hope shattered. Alice lay there, her arms wrapped protectively around James Jr. Harper's knees buckled, and he sank beside them, cradling their lifeless forms. His hands trembled, slick with blood. This was his brutal reality.

In that haunting moment, Harper was adrift in a sea of memories. Clinging to their bodies, his gaze lingered on the familiar setting of Alice's room. He recalled James Jr.'s infectious laughter during hide-and-seek games, always choosing the worst hiding spots and unable to stifle his giggles inside the closet. Alice's tea party setup, with beloved stuffed animals each bearing distinct personalities, now stood as a poignant reminder of innocence lost.

Their posture recalled a memory in vivid detail. It was a chilly afternoon at the playground, and Harper had been watching from a distance. James Jr., with his gentle nature, had become the target of a group of bullies. They surrounded him, mocking and pushing him around the playground. A surge of emotion gripped Harper, urging him to intervene, but he paused as he witnessed Alice step up. Despite being smaller, she placed herself between James Jr. and the bullies, her eyes fierce and her stance unwavering. She spoke firmly, defending her brother with a courage that belied her age. The bullies hesitated, then backed off, muttering under their breaths. James looked at Alice with a mixture of relief and admiration, and Harper felt a swell of pride. She had always been James Jr.'s protector, always looking out for her little brother with an unbreakable bond, standing by him until the very end.

He closed his eyes, desperately wishing to awaken from this nightmare. Yet, the cold, harsh reality pierced through—a hellish awakening.

As he knelt, clutching his children's lifeless bodies, a profound realization swept over him like an icy tide—life would never be the same. His vibrant world, once whole and full of promise, now lay in ruins, shattered like shards of glass strewn across the ground.

The living room succumbed to darkness, mirroring the bleakness engulfing his heart. So be it, he thought, his journey into the abyss would be fueled by an insatiable need for vengeance.

Harper's gaze fixed on the motionless figures of his wife and children beside the spent fireplace, where the fire's warmth once mirrored the life within his family. Torment, disbelief, and rage collided within him, each emotion struggling for dominance, yearning for release. The agony was unbearable, but it was the last sensation grounding him to reality. Every fiber of his soul burned with a relentless thirst for vengeance. His quest for justice was unbound by the constraints of the law. The trespassers had inflicted upon him a life of emptiness, one he now demanded they repay with their own lives. This reckoning was etched in the stone of fate, where blood would pay for blood.

Sitting on the living room floor, memories of their life together flooded Harper's mind—the laughter, the love, the dreams they once shared. All of it was gone, snuffed out in an instant. His heart ached with a pain he had never known, and a cold resolve began to take root. The darkness became his eternal companion, one that would guide him unerringly on a path for revenge.

Sirens echoed outside, the red and blue lights flashing through the windows of Harper's house. The rain had ceased, but brooding, ominous clouds still loomed overhead, casting a malevolent shadow over the home. Harper stood immobile, his eyes riveted on the gaping front door. Inside, the walls and doors bore silent witness to the consuming tragedy.

"Foundry Hills Police Department!" a voice boomed from outside. Two officers, pistols drawn and eyes sharp, cautiously approached the front door, their movements deliberate and tense.

"I am Officer Matthews with the Foundry Hills Police Department. Show me your hands!" His authoritative tone cut through the air, but Harper did not move, paralyzed by shock and grief.

Matthews exchanged a quick glance with his partner, Officer Peters. "Cover him while I clear the house," Matthews instructed, his voice low and urgent.

"Copy that," Peters replied, keeping his weapon trained on Harper while Matthews moved forward.

Matthews advanced methodically, his steps careful and precise as he swept through each room, checking for any remaining threats. Peters maintained his position, his eyes darting between Harper and the rest of the house.

The minutes felt like hours, the tension thick in the air. Matthews returned, shaking his head slightly to indicate the house was clear. He holstered his weapon and approached Harper slowly, his expression softening.

"Sir, can you hear me?" Matthews asked, kneeling beside Harper, his voice gentler now. "We're here to help. Can you tell me what happened?"

Harper's surroundings blurred, the officers' voices fading in and out. The shock and despair enveloped him, rendering him almost catatonic. The movements of the officers seemed fast-forwarded, a whirlwind of activity in a world that had slowed to a crawl.

Peters called for backup and medical assistance, the urgency evident in his voice. "We need paramedics at 113 Warren Court. Multiple injuries, possible fatalities."

Harper barely registered their actions, his mind numb and his body unresponsive. The officers' efforts to communicate felt distant, their words lost in the overwhelming fog of his trauma.

Pain consumed him, radiating from the brutal strikes to his head. Reality felt like it was slipping away. His sight grew hazy, narrowing into a dark tunnel. Each breath became labored, his chest heaving as his body struggled to keep up. Thoughts grew sluggish as a heavy fog descended upon them. Everything became a blur, and the throbbing in his head grew stronger, overpowering all other sensations. As the earth seemed to sway beneath him, Harper felt his strength wane. With one last trembling exhale, he succumbed to the darkness.

CHAPTER 3: DETECTIVE ANDREWS

The smell of chimney smoke and dirt filled Detective Shawn Andrews' nostrils as he stood outside his undercover patrol vehicle. The block of Warren Court was illuminated by the harsh glare of emergency lights under a grim sky. Neighbors huddled by their doors, faces etched with curiosity and fear. The wood-burning smoke drifted through the air, mingling with the acrid scent of destruction. Glass from the shattered front door glittered on the ground like ominous confetti. Andrews carefully stepped inside, the crunch of glass under his heels drawing the analysts' attention.

Retrieving a handkerchief from his coat, Andrews pressed it to his nose to block out the faint scent of death. The victims had been dead for only a few hours, but the smell was already suffocating. Blood splatter marred the carpet and walls, revealing a scene of grotesque violence. Popcorn and a laptop lay on the floor, covered in bits of brain matter and blood. Andrews' expression remained stoic.

He moved cautiously, his eyes scanning for any clues that might help piece together the night's events. He noticed Emily Berg leaning over with an evidence bag. Her auburn hair, neatly tied in a low bun, framed her face. Her eyes, a striking blue, resembled the wings of a Menelaus blue morpho butterfly. The combination of her tailored navy blazer and white blouse exuded professionalism and sophistication.

"Emily," he nodded. "What are we dealing with here?"

"The male victim was found on the ground, alive, with multiple blunt injuries to the head, clutching his family. Unfortunately, the rest of the family weren't as fortunate—fatal gunshot wounds for all:

the adult female was shot in the side of the head, the boy in the back of the head, and the girl the same as the boy. Based on evidence found in the girl's closet, it appears the children were most likely brought out here by the adult male victim," she said, her gaze fixed on the body bags.

"That's terrible. I can't even imagine being in his shoes. Do we have any leads on the suspects?" Andrews asked, his voice heavy with concern.

Emily shook her head. "No, there's been no other evidence or leads so far. We've spoken to neighbors on both sides of the house. One of them called 911 when they heard the gunshots. By the time they looked out their window, a dark SUV was already leaving the area."

"Of course," Andrews sighed irritably, "nobody ever seems to know or see anything useful to assist law enforcement here in Foundry Hills."

"No obvious motive either. Looking into Mr. Harper's profession, he works at Foundry TechUse as a cybersecurity analyst. I plan on going up there and asking questions in the morning."

"Sounds good. Anything else?" he asked.

"Just this, found it near their bodies."

Emily handed Andrews an initial report and evidence bag. He lifted the bag, peering at its contents—a box labeled "For my love" and a gold necklace with an emerald pendant.

"Maybe it was an anniversary gift of some sort? I will take it for now." Andrews placed the bag into his coat pocket. "Good work. I'm going to look around and see if there's anything we may have missed," he said, walking deeper into the living space.

He paused by the family photos on the mantle above the fireplace, his gaze lingering on the smiling faces that now felt like ghosts staring back. It was difficult to reconcile this image of a loving family with the horrific scene before him. He felt a deep sense of injustice; Warren Court had never been victim to such horror. And why leave a survivor? Did it have something to do with Harper? Andrews crouched beside the spot where Harper had been found, on his knees holding his lifeless family close. Harper had sustained a couple of blunt injuries, but nothing compared to the extent of those around him. It was almost as if they wanted him to live, to suffer the torment of surviving when his loved ones didn't. Or perhaps they had a different reason.

Andrews made his way through the house, his footsteps echoing softly on the hardwood floors. The children's rooms appeared tidy and organized. Inside Alice's closet, clothes hung neatly, a row of sneakers and a backpack labeled A.H arranged on the floor. Crime scene tags marked spots of blood along the back wall and carpet, clear indications that part of the tragedies of this evening unfolded here.

Emily entered the room and approached Andrews. "Detective, the medical examiner team is ready to take the bodies," she said softly, her eyes reflecting the shared sorrow of the moment.

Andrews nodded, returning to the living area. His gaze followed as the gurneys carrying Denise, Alice, and James Jr. were wheeled out the door. "Make sure everything is documented thoroughly," he instructed. "We need all the information we can get to find out who did this and why."

Emily nodded and left the house to coordinate with the team. Andrews followed suit, each step splashing in puddles on the damp pavement slick with rain. The turbulence and rush of water in the creek beside the house drew his attention, the water spilling over its banks.

He opened the door to his sleek sporty sedan and slid into the plush leather seats. The engine purred to life, filling the quiet with a steady hum. Andrews paused, his eyes drawn to the roiling creek nearby, pondering the unsettling question: why had Harper been spared?

The drive back home from Warren Court required a brief detour—a quick stop at a nearby convenience store. Andrews entered with purpose, noting the scent of floor cleaning solution as he left faint moody footprints on the linoleum floor. He made his way to the counter where the cashier, a young man named George with a friendly demeanor, was waiting.

"Evening George, sorry about the floor," Andrews apologized.

"Don't worry about it, Shawn," George replied, keying in the purchase on the register. "What happened up the road? I saw all those crime scene vehicles driving up."

Andrews wavered for a moment, then replied vaguely, "Just another incident. My team is handling it."

The cashier nodded, scanning the product. "Just $18.99," he said, placing it into a bag.

"Here you go, George, keep the change," Andrews replied, taking the bag and heading back to his vehicle.

Driving away, he merged onto the expressway, taking the exit three ramps later. Finally, he arrived at his home, retrieving the item from the bag. As he glanced at his reflection in the rearview mirror, he saw a man with a clean-shaven face, black hair neatly styled with a sharp sideways part, and faint lines etched around his eyes. Andrews twisted the cap off and took a drink, the liquid warming him as he pondered the dark puzzle before him.

Chapter 4: Concussion Protocol

In the hospital bed, the sterile scent of disinfectant filled the room, accompanied by the steady beep of a monitor beside him. This visit felt vastly different from his previous ones. This time, he was alone, without the uplifting presence of Denise, Alice, or James.

He remembered the occasions they had visited here together—three times for Denise, twice for the joyful arrivals of their children, Alice and James. The third visit followed a freak accident where Denise fractured her knee, an injury that tested their marriage as she spent eight months bedridden in recovery.

There was also the time they brought Alice in; she had a severe bout of scarlet fever. After multiple high fevers and infections, the doctors determined that her tonsils were to blame. Their removal finally put an end to her frequent illnesses. James, their resilient and courageous boy, had once cut his head deeply after snapping a laundry basket during a playful session with his sister. Fortunately, it only left a small scar.

As he looked around the hospital room, his eyes began to tear up. The quiet, cold environment only heightened his sense of isolation. The walls, painted a dull, lifeless off-white, closed in on him, intensifying his suffocating grief. Every breath felt labored, each inhalation a reminder that he was alone.

A faint echo of footsteps approached. A man in his mid-40s entered the room, his white coat crisp and clean, a stethoscope draped around his neck.

"Mr. James Harper?" he said, his voice calm. He looked up from the chart, his eyes meeting Harper's with gentle concern. "I'm Dr.

Evans, one of the attending physicians here at Foundry Hills Medical Center. How are you feeling?"

The question lingered in the air as the pain in James' head radiated through his entire body. The weight of his loss, the emptiness that had taken root in his chest, was all-consuming. He knew Dr. Evans was just doing his job, but how could he articulate the depths of his sorrow, the profound ache that words seemed inadequate to express?

"A bit of a headache," he murmured, the words escaping his lips, a mere acknowledgment of the anchored desolation.

Dr. Evans' eyes reflected empathy as he carefully set the chart aside. "That's understandable. Take it one day at a time."

He took a moment to let his words sink in, then took a deep breath before continuing. "On a more immediate note, Harper, I need to inform you that the medical team that transported you here observed several blunt traumas to your head during their assessment. Given the nature of these injuries, it's crucial that we closely monitor you for signs of concussion and any other possible complications. We'll be following a concussion protocol, which entails regular neurological assessments and vigilant monitoring for symptoms like headaches, dizziness, nausea, and changes in cognitive function. It's crucial that you take it easy and avoid any strenuous activities until we can be certain there are no lingering effects."

He paused, then continued thoughtfully, "Physically, you're healing, but emotionally, it will take time. I heard what happened to you, and your grief is another wound that needs tending. It's a journey, James, like navigating through an uncharted wilderness. Some days, the path will be clear, and other days, you'll feel utterly lost. It's not something you can rush through or push aside. Some days will be harder than others, and that's okay. The important thing is to allow yourself to feel, to process each emotion as it comes. Lean on those around you, let them support you."

Harper's gaze fell to his hands, clenched tightly in his lap as he absorbed Dr. Evans' words. His voice was strained, laden with grief and a hint of frustration. "Dr. Evans, I... I appreciate everything you're doing. But when can I go home? I need to be there."

"I'm sorry, Harper, I really am. But we need to keep you here for a couple of days to ensure you're recovering properly," Dr. Evans said gently.

With a comforting nod, he returned his attention to the screen, his practiced hands navigating through the patient data. "Your vital signs are stable at the moment, but given the severity of your head trauma, we'll need to monitor you closely for any changes," he said, his voice conveying compassion. "Concussions can be tricky, and it's crucial to watch out for its symptoms."

As Dr. Evans' words washed over him, barely registering, the physical pain was nothing compared to the torture that gnawed at his soul. All he could think about was the gaping void where his family once was. The reality of his survival felt like a cruel joke.

A knock on the hospital room door drew Harper's attention. Dr. Evans glanced at the door, then back at Harper. "I'll see who that is," he said before stepping out.

A moment later, Dr. Evans returned, followed by a man in a neat suit. A badge gleamed on his belt line, a firearm holstered at his side. His attire—a crisp blue button-down shirt and sharp slacks—spoke of professionalism. Yet, his expression carried a subtle empathy, a quality tempered by years of witnessing both tragedy and resolve.

"Mr. Harper? Good morning, I am Detective Andrews with the Foundry Hills Police Department. How are you feeling?" he asked genuinely, his voice soft yet authoritative.

Another person asking the same question, as if the answer would somehow make everything better. But how could it?

"I'm okay, Detective. Have you found anything on my family's killers?" Harper asked, hoping for a sliver of progress.

"Unfortunately, nothing at the moment. I was wondering if you wouldn't mind if I ask you several questions about last night?" Andrews continued.

Dr. Evans gave a supportive nod. "I'll give you some time to talk. A nurse will be back later to check on you," he said before departing the room, leaving them alone.

Harper struggled to summon the energy to respond. The words felt heavy, buried deep within his grief. "What do you want to know?" he managed weakly.

Andrews pulled a chair closer to the bed, his eyes scanning Harper's face for any sign of recognition. "Mr. Harper, can you tell me anything about the suspects that entered your home? Anything out of the ordinary?"

Harper met the detective's gaze, wondering if the man had ever experienced the profound loss he was enduring. Did he comprehend the pain and rage festering inside him, his overwhelming desire for solitude, and the knowledge that seeing the intruders in jail would never satisfy the justice he yearned for? He wanted them in a wooden bed, six feet under.

Fragmented memories surged back and forth within Harper like a relentless tide, threatening to engulf him. The trauma was fresh and raw. He closed his eyes, trying to piece together the horrific night.

"I remember... three of them wearing masks," Harper began, his voice strained. "All armed, moving about like shadows. They were... coordinated, like they had killed without regret."

Andrews nodded, jotting down notes. "Anything else? Any other distinguishing features, accents, anything at all?"

Harper's mind raced, the faces of his assailants emerging from the darkness. "The first intruder was tall with a muscular build. The second was smaller but agile, his movements quick. The third, the one who held my wife at gunpoint, had a gaze that felt like it was the end for me and my family. They were professionals. One had a tattoo, something resembling an eclipse on his hand," Harper said, his voice growing stronger as the details came back.

Andrews leaned in, his interest piqued. "Did they say anything? Anything that might hint at their motive or identity?"

Harper shook his head slightly, trying to recall. "Not much. They were quiet."

Detective Andrews jotted down more notes, then looked up. "You mentioned that tattoo... Harper, have you heard of the Nightshade Organization?"

Harper frowned, shaking his head again. "I've heard the name. I know they operate in Foundry Hills and commit organized crime. But I don't know why they would target me or what it has to do with the tattoo."

Andrews nodded thoughtfully. "The Nightshade Organization is more than just a gang. They have their hands in a lot of illegal activities, and that tattoo you mentioned is one of their symbols."

Harper's eyes widened slightly. "I had no idea. Why would they come after me?"

"That's what we need to figure out," Andrews replied. "Your information is helpful, though. It gives us a lead to follow."

Andrews' eyes softened with sympathy, but he kept his professional detachment. "Harper, I promise we will do everything we can to bring them to justice. Your cooperation is crucial in helping us catch the ones responsible."

"I appreciate that, Detective," Harper replied.

"Listen, I have something for you that I hope will help in your grieving." He reached into his pocket and pulled out an evidence bag. "I've been doing this for a while, and I know when something is of value in evidence or not. Here, one of my team members found this. I felt it was right to return it to you." He handed Harper the bag.

Harper opened the bag and reached inside, retrieving an emerald necklace and pendant. His face frowned, and his eyes squinted as he tried to hold back his tears. "Thank you, Detective. This... this means a lot to me," Harper said, looking at the contents.

"You're welcome, Harper. I'll be reaching out soon."

They both shared a nod as Andrews left the room, leaving Harper alone with his thoughts. The room's cold, sterile environment fed into his isolation, and the desire for vengeance burned brighter with each passing second, fueled by the green shine of the pendant reflecting at him.

The pendant was a gift he had planned to give Denise the night his family was murdered. Its green sparkle reminded him of her eyes, twinkling like emeralds. He closed his eyes, a sweet dream of her playing in his mind.

***

Needing a guide to assist him with his work, Harper entered the Foundry Bookstore. His eyes scanned the store for the self-help section, and there it was on the left, near the coffee shop. On his way, his attention was caught by a red-headed woman whose long hair cascaded to the middle of her back. She turned and caught him looking at her, causing him to bump into a table. She smiled as he continued to make his way behind the book aisle.

Several days later, Harper saw her again, sitting at a table engrossed in a book. "I see you skipped the coffee," he said jokingly.

"I did. Figured, why not give the books a try," she smiled.

Fate would have it that there were no other seats available. "May I?" he asked, gesturing to the chair. She nodded, "Please."

Her gaze remained fixed on the open pages of her book. A breeze carried her scent towards him—a faint fragrance that he would later recognize as Chanel. Adjusting his glasses, Harper felt a strange sensation in his chest, a mix of nervousness and excitement. Unable to help himself, he glanced at her, and their eyes met.

For a moment, time seemed to stand still. He would never forget her gentle green eyes, those beautiful, captivating enigmas. Despite their disparate reasons for being there, destiny had conspired to bring them together that day and forever after.

***

The eclipse tattoo was a start; it was a tangible lead in the pursuit of justice for his family. And the necklace, wrapped around his hand as he clenched the pendant tightly, turning his knuckles white, was a symbol of his determination that he was not willing to let go or forgive.

He couldn't leave this to the authorities; he had to, wanted to take matters into his own hands. The journey was filled with uncertainty, but he was undiscouraged. He owed it to Denise, Alice, and James Jr. to uncover the truth, to ensure that their deaths were not in vain.

A knock at the door distracted Harper from his mental scheming. Sam and Greg, his coworkers from the office, came to visit, their eyes red-rimmed. They entered with a bouquet of white lilies. Both were as awkward as Harper in their own way, much like him—introverted cybersecurity analysts who preferred the company of code over people. Today, however, their discomfort was overshadowed by the grief they shared with him. They had known Denise, Alice, and James well from the annual holiday dinners, especially the Thanksgiving potlucks where the company's families would come together. Denise's pumpkin cheesecake was a highlight, a treat that made everyone in the office drool, something they always looked forward to.

"James," Sam began, his voice unsteady, "we are so sorry, we can't even begin to understand what you're going through. Everyone at the TechUse office sends their deepest condolences. We are all thinking of you."

Greg nodded, his eyes moist with unshed tears. "We were all so fond of Denise and the kids. They were like family to us. Alice always brought that infectious energy to the Thanksgiving potlucks, remember? She would run around with the other kids, organizing games and making everyone laugh. And James Jr.... he always had questions about our work. They were special, James. Truly special."

Their words drifted Harper back to a recollection of James Jr.'s insightful question on Artificial Intelligence, an area where Harper's talent was very keen.

***

In the modern conference room, Harper stood before a group of professionals, including some high-profile uniformed visitors from the state and federal levels. Among them was Mr. Ivan Seraphin, famous for his leadership tenure in SynTech Intelligence Systems (SIS), an organization researching the capabilities of AI. He had recently taken over as head of TechUse.

"Today, I'll demonstrate how AI can revolutionize our approach to cybersecurity," Harper began, his voice steady. He scanned the audience. "I need a volunteer."

After a moment of hesitation, a woman in the second row raised her hand. "I'll volunteer," she said, standing up. She introduced herself as Sarah Collins, a mid-level manager in the IT department.

"Thank you, Sarah," Harper said with a nod. "Please come up to the stage."

Sarah made her way to the front, a mix of curiosity and nervousness on her face. Harper gestured for her to stand next to him. He then turned to the audience.

"Using the AI program we've developed, I'll retrieve public and private information about Sarah in real-time," he explained. "This will demonstrate the speed and accuracy of our system."

Harper typed a few commands into his laptop, and within moments, data began to populate the screen. The audience leaned forward, murmurs of amazement spreading through the room.

"Sarah Collins," Harper read aloud from the screen, "age 34, graduated from MIT with a degree in computer science, currently employed at the Department of Defense as an IT manager. Lives in Arlington, Virginia, with her husband and two children. She recently spent $100 at a retail shop two hours ago."

Sarah's eyes widened. "That's incredible," she said, staring at the screen displaying her personal details. The crowd reacted with both astonishment and concern, whispering among themselves.

Harper smiled, adjusting his glasses. "Our AI system scours any and all databases and cross-references the data with astonishing speed and accuracy. It can compile a comprehensive profile in seconds."

The audience erupted in whispered conversations, clearly impressed by the demonstration but also uneasy about the implications. Seraphin, seated in the front row, leaned forward with keen interest.

Another attendee raised a hand. "Is this level of detail typical for all individuals?"

"Yes," Harper replied. "Our system is designed to handle vast amounts of data, making it a powerful tool for cybersecurity and information gathering."

A concerned voice from the back called out, "What about privacy? Isn't this kind of access dangerous and a violation of people's rights?"

Harper held up a hand to calm the room. "I understand your concerns. As the system's creator, I have implemented strict controls. The use of this technology is regulated, and we have the ability to turn off and control its access based on its intended use. Your privacy and security are paramount."

The audience seemed to relax slightly, though the concern was still evident. After the presentation, as the audience buzzed with astonishment, Seraphin approached him. His handshake was firm, his smile warm yet calculated. "James, that was truly impressive," he said, his voice smooth and authoritative. "Your ability to gather and analyze information in real-time is nothing short of revolutionary."

Harper nodded modestly. "Thank you, Mr. Seraphin. I believe AI has the potential to shape the future in profound ways."

"Indeed, it does," Seraphin replied, his eyes gleaming with a hint of something deeper. "The work you're doing could change everything. With the right resources and support, your talents could be used for even greater purposes."

Sam and Greg looked at him, confused. "Hey, are you okay?" Greg asked, concern evident in his voice.

Harper blinked, shaking off the remnants of the vivid recollection. "Yeah, I must have dosed off for a moment," he replied, trying to refocus on the present.

"We were saying not to worry about anything back at TechUse. We've got things covered," Sam continued, trying to maintain a steady voice. "Take the time you need, Greg and I will manage."

Greg added, "Yeah, we're handling the project. It's tough without you, but we're holding up. We want you to focus on yourself right now."

Despite their attempts to be supportive, the depth of his sorrow was insurmountable. They hesitated, exchanging glances as if debating whether to bring up work at all.

"What is it?" Harper asked, sensing they were holding something back. After working with these two for years, he could always tell when they were stumped on something.

Sam finally spoke up, his voice hesitant. "We've been stuck on this piece of code for weeks, but we don't want to burden you with it right now."

Harper looked at their worried faces and insisted, needing the distraction. "Show me. Maybe it will help take my mind off things for a bit."

Greg pulled out his phone, opening an app where he had snippets of the code saved. "We've been stuck on this for a while," he admitted, scrolling through the lines of code. "We isolated the problem to this segment, but we just can't figure out what's going wrong. Every time we run it, it throws an error."

Sam chimed in, "We thought we had it fixed last night, but the same bug keeps popping up. We even double-checked the logic and the syntax, but something's not clicking."

Greg continued, "We're pretty sure the issue is somewhere in these lines, but we're too close to see it. We were hoping you could take a look and maybe point out what we're missing."

Handing him the phone, they watched as he glanced over the code. It was difficult to focus through the haze of grief, but as he scanned the familiar lines, he noticed a small but critical error. "Here," he said, pointing to a variable that had been incorrectly initialized. "This should be an array, not a single value. That's why your loop is failing."

Both stared at the screen, their faces lighting up with recognition. "Wow," Sam said. "You're remarkable, Harper. Even in your current state, you can spot these things."

Harper managed a faint smile. It felt good to be helpful, even if only for a moment.

They spent the next couple of hours catching up and discussing work as the sun set. As visiting hours came to an end, a nurse entered and gently reminded them it was time to leave. Sam and Greg stood up, their reluctance to go evident in their slow movements.

"We'll be back to check on you, Harper," Sam said, placing a hand on his shoulder. "Remember, we're here for you, no matter what."

"Yeah, and if you need anything, don't hesitate to reach out," Greg added, giving him a small, encouraging smile.

Harper nodded, appreciating their efforts. He watched them leave.

Left alone, Harper thought about the code he had just debugged, which seemed trivial compared to the gaping void left by his family's absence.

Tears welled up in his eyes as he thought about the simple, everyday moments he would miss—the bedtime stories, the weekend outings, the family dinners. He missed Denise's touch, her presence, the way she always knew how to make everything better.

He closed his eyes, hoping that when he opened them again, he would awaken from this nightmare, but he didn't. Each blink was a struggle to keep them open until he finally succumbed to sleep.

In his dreams, his family was alive. They were back in their living room, the warm glow of the fireplace casting a comforting light across the room. Denise sat on the couch, laughing at something. Alice danced around the room, her giggles blending harmoniously with James Jr.'s excited chatter about his toys and video games.

But the dream quickly morphed into a nightmare. The warm light of the fireplace flickered and died. The room grew darker, and the familiar sounds of joy were replaced by the terrifying echoes of that horrific night. The shattering of glass, the sudden, violent intrusion of the armed men, Denise's scream piercing the night—it all replayed in intense detail, each moment etched vividly in his mind. Harper felt the brutal blow to his head again, the searing pain that followed.

He bolted upright in the dark, his heart pounding, and his vitals off the charts. Sweat drenched his body, and his breath came in ragged gasps. Two nurses rushed in, switching on the lights, their faces filled with urgency. They moved swiftly, their practiced hands working to calm him. One nurse gently pressed him back against the bed while the other prepared a syringe.

"Mr. Harper, you need to calm down," one of them said, her voice soothing but firm. "You're safe here."

The other nurse injected him with a sedative, and slowly, the world around him began to fade. The sharp edges of his panic dulled, and the oppressive weight on his chest lightened. The room grew blurry, the nurses' faces becoming indistinct shapes as the sedative took effect. He felt himself sinking back into the bed, the darkness enveloping him once more.

***

After a couple of days, Harper was finally discharged from the hospital. Dr. Evans entered the room, holding a clipboard. "Good news, Harper," he said, smiling gently. "The tests show no signs of a concussion."

Harper nodded, feeling slight relief.

"However," Dr. Evans continued, his tone more serious, "the trauma may significantly impact your mental state. It's important to address this as part of your recovery."

He handed him a referral. "This is for a specialist. Please seek further care within the next week."

Harper took the referral, glancing at the paperwork. His eyes skimmed over the diagnosis: 'Post-Traumatic Stress Disorder due to Homicidal Trauma.' It felt surreal reading those words—a clinical label for the unrestrained emotions consuming him. The sterile language couldn't capture the depth of the pain, the relentless waves of grief and anger crashing over him. Each letter felt like a stab to the heart, a cruel reminder of the reality he was now living.

As he walked out of the patient room, he glanced at the other patients, each enduring their own form of torment. Some lay motionless, lost in their battles, while others stared blankly at the ceiling, their eyes reflecting a shared suffering.

In the elevator, he stood silently, clutching a bag containing his belongings from that night. The weight of the bag seemed to pull him down, each item a tangible reminder of the life that had been violently ripped away from him.

The elevator ride felt interminable, the silence thick with unspoken pain. As the doors slid open, he was greeted by the busy sounds of the hospital lobby. Families reunited, laughter and tears mingling. The sight tore at his heart, a bitter reminder of the happiness that had been stolen from him.

The elevator stopped, and an elderly man entered, joyfully discussing the arrival of his newborn grandson on the phone.

"He's absolutely perfect," the grandfather said, his voice brimming with pride. "Born just three nights ago. He's a little bundle of joy."

Harper's heart sank as he listened to the conversation. The man continued, oblivious to Harper's pain.

"Yes, I'm on my way to see him now," the grandfather said. "I can't wait to hold him. He's going to have so many stories from his grandpa."

His family had been taken from him the very same night this baby was born. Such was the unyielding rhythm of life—where new beginnings emerged as others tragically met their end.

The grandfather noticed Harper standing silently in the corner and offered a warm smile. "Do you have grandchildren?" he asked kindly.

Harper forced a smile, his heart aching. "No," he replied softly. "But that is a cute baby."

"He is," the grandfather agreed warmly.

Harper nodded, trying to keep his voice steady. "It's alright. It's good to see new life bringing so much joy."

The grandfather's eyes reflected deep sympathy. "If you ever need someone to talk to, sometimes sharing helps," he offered gently, his own excitement now tempered by Harper's evident pain.

Their interaction underscored the contrast between the grandfather's joy and Harper's despair, illustrating life's indifferent cycle. As the elevator doors opened in the lobby, the grandfather exited and Harper followed behind him. The revolving doors revealed another rainy day in Foundry Hills. A somber gray sky reflected his grief, the raindrops mirroring the tears he could no longer shed. The city was cloaked in a melancholy drizzle, the streets slick and glistening under the dim light.

The hustle and bustle of Foundry Hills pressed on, apathetic to the incident that turned his life upside down. People hurried by, umbrellas shielding them from the rain, their faces blurred and distant. Nearby, the metro rumbled, carrying passengers to and from the heart of the city. In the distance, the smokestacks of the industrial district loomed, factories tirelessly churning out plumes of smoke. Rolling Peaks, the high elevated town, stood watch over the city, its peaks shrouded in mist.

As Harper stepped out into the rain, the oppressive weight of the city pressed down on him. His thoughts drifted to the idea of cosmic balance, but it brought no comfort. He had just lost his family; the notion of balance felt hollow and cruel. The interconnectedness of joy and suffering was a bitter reminder that for every life taken, another might be given, but it did nothing to fill the void within him.

Instead, a burning desire for retribution surged, the urge to become his own arbiter of justice smoldering deep inside. His thoughts were consumed not by balance, but by vengeance. This battle was far from over; it had only just begun.

CHAPTER 5: THE ECLIPSE TATTOO

The taxi approached Warren Court, a neighborhood Harper never knew he'd dread returning to. Its headlights cut through the darkness of adjacent driveways before coming to a final stop down the street. From the vehicle, Harper observed the police tape still on the door of what once hid and kept the love inside. Now, the entrance acted as a barrier, keeping him out while the shadows hid inside.

Upon paying the driver and stepping out of the taxi's rear seat, he was met with the sound of the wind howling, as if it was a divine warning. An officer patrolled the entrance, keeping a watchful eye to prevent any tampering with the evidence within the scene. Harper knew he had to exercise caution if he wished to gain access to the house.

The crime scene remained active; professional cleaners had taken the evening off after tirelessly toiling to erase the traces of his nightmare. Still, he knew no amount of cleaning could purge the emotional scars it had left behind.

He made his way behind a nearby bush, waiting patiently for the guard to make his rounds. As predicted, the guard made his way to the back of the house, his flashlight leading the way. Harper glided with agility and stealth across the driveway, reaching the front window and carefully prying it open. Delicately, he shifted a potted plant, ensuring silence was his sole companion.

Once inside, he secured the window and released the curtain back to its place. Noise from the air conditioner and electronic devices welcomed him. The living room, once occupied with laughter and joy, was now vacant except for the cerise stains he knelt before. As he glanced around, the photos, furniture, and decor all mocked him of a life he could never reclaim.

Harper navigated through the house, each room a minefield of memories. Denise's essence lingered in the kitchen, summoning images of their morning rituals—sipping coffee as the kids left for school. Harper walked over to the table, running his hand across the espresso-stained surface that had hosted a thousand meals. It felt almost like yesterday that he would hear Denise hum enchanting tunes as she cooked, the scent lifting his children off their feet—a sensation never to return. Yet, a faint fragrance of her perfume remained, casting ghostly echoes of her presence beside him.

Venture into the children's bedrooms, the floorboards creaked under each step. Alice's laughter and steps resonated through the halls, a pursuit from embrace that he would never be able to do again. In the halls, he recalled James Jr.'s chubby legs trembling as he toddled toward Denise, his first steps into their world. He smiled, but as he did, the visions of happiness dissipated like phantoms, retreating into the dark corners of his mind, leaving behind nothing but despair.

Hesitantly, Harper walked into Alice's pink-walled sanctuary, a color she begged for on her 10th birthday. The bed was carefully arranged with a variety of stuffed animals, each holding its own cherished place in her heart. Among them was her favorite companion since she was five, a well-loved teddy bear she affectionately named Mr. Flufferson, its vibrant fur faded with the passage of time. Her vanity mirror, a gift passed down by Denise, forever holding its secrets of their shared moments.

James Jr.'s room, a toy-filled sanctuary, was a childhood haven Harper wished he'd had. The comic book library, meticulously alphabetized and orderly, was a prized collection that James Jr. promised to cherish and expand as he grew older. Action figures and beloved toys set up on display on the shelves, silently mourning their young owner.

The stark reality that neither of his children would experience the joys of adulthood weighed heavily on Harper. They would never drive their first car, earn their first paycheck, or navigate the challenges of adulthood. The thought lanced at his heart; each unfulfilled dream of the future had been stolen from them.

He continued through the house, pausing at the entryway to their bedroom, where he and Denise had shared their dreams. Their once intimate king-sized retreat now lay cold and abandoned, its soft sheets and plush pillows no longer offering the comfort they once did. Collapsing onto the bed, Harper was consumed by a sense of defeat, overwhelmed by loss.

A darker thought crept in, whispering the possibility of escape, of ending it all. The enormity of his loss made the idea seem almost inviting. Yet, even in the depths of his despair, he knew he couldn't succumb to such a final act. Despite the overwhelming pain, a flicker of hope still burned within him, a stubborn ember refusing to be doused. He clung to it, knowing that giving up would mean letting go of the love and memories that still sustained him.

His vision blurred, and the room seemed to shift, its walls closing in as a cold sweat broke out on his forehead. He blinked, trying to clear his sight, but instead, the room morphed into a different scene.

The living room materialized around him. Denise was there, her form shimmering like an apparition. She looked at him with a mixture of sorrow and love, her eyes deep pools of emotion that seemed to reach into his very soul.

Alice and James Jr. were playing nearby, filling Harper with a warmth he hadn't felt since the night of the tragedy. "Denise?" Harper whispered. He reached out, but his hand passed through her.

Denise's lips curved into a sad smile, her eyes glistening with unspoken sorrow. "We're here, Harper. We will always be here," she said, her voice distant. "You have to be strong."

The children's laughter grew louder, almost cacophonous. The vision started to fade, and he desperately tried to hold onto it, but the more he reached out, the faster it dissipated.

Like a dream, he was back in the cold, empty bedroom, his heart pounding, his breath coming in shallow gasps. He sat up, rubbing his eyes, trying to dispel the remnants of the hallucination. What was happening to him? Was he losing his mind? The room, free of the ethereal glow, felt even colder and more desolate than before.

Shaking off the disorienting vision, Harper was suddenly frozen by a beam of light shining through the window. It was the patrolling officer. Harper stood perfectly still, barely daring to breathe, until the officer moved on. After the coast was clear, he quietly sneaked back out of the house, careful to avoid the guard.

Walking away from the house toward the nearby creek, Harper crouched by the edge, watching the stream wind through the rocks and debris. As he observed the steady current, a sense of purpose began to clear his mind. The eclipse tattoo—the symbol of his tormentors—became his focus. It was the crucial piece of the puzzle he needed to unravel.

***

Detective Andrews wasted no time at the Foundry Hills Police Department, pursuing the lead to Harper's case. The crimson eclipse tattoo was a symbol renowned among the leaders of the Nightshade organization. The investigations floor was heavy with activity. In the detective's area, one wall was specifically dedicated to Nightshade's hierarchy and operations. At the top of the board were photos of the three families: Cartwright, Vargas, and Delgado, each controlling their own territory and unique areas of crime within Foundry Hills. Another criminal organization, the White Dagger Triad (WDT), existed but had not made enough noise to warrant the attention of Detective Andrews and his team. None of the WDT members bore the tattoo in question for the case, and they were not considered a significant criminal threat.

In the criminal underworld of Foundry Hills, the notorious families held power over various illegal enterprises, each one contributing to a network of crime that beset the city. Detective Andrews stared at the wall, his thoughts on the first interaction with James Harper at the hospital. Harper's haunted eyes and fierce determination had left a mark on him. The man had lost everything, except the fire that scorched in his eyes. They were the eyes of a man driven by vengeance, something Andrews couldn't ignore.

Detective Andrews shifted his focus back to the investigation, his eyes scanning the photographs and maps pinned to the board. At the top of the criminal hierarchy was Hector Cartwright, the ruthless patriarch of the Cartwright family. Andrews traced a line on the map with his finger, following the drug routes that extended through the industrial district. Hector's operations spanned a network of warehouses and factories where heroin and cocaine were manufactured and distributed. His extensive network of distributors ensured that his products reached every corner of Foundry Hills and beyond. The Cartwrights maintained their grip on the drug market through a combination of fear, bribery, and strategic alliances with corrupt officials.

Hector, always several steps ahead of law enforcement, meticulously planned his operations. Layers of intermediaries and cutouts made it nearly impossible for authorities to trace anything back to him directly. The Cartwrights used state-of-the-art technology to monitor their operations and communications, frequently changing methods and locations to evade detection. Hector's influence extended beyond the drug trade, with investments in legitimate businesses providing a veneer of respectability and a steady stream of laundered money.

Isabella Vargas, the matriarch of the Vargas family, oversaw a sinister human trafficking operation centered around the docks near Foundry Hills. Andrews moved to another section of the board, where a map was marked with key locations. Isabella's legitimate shipping business served as a front for smuggling humans into and out of the city. Her network relied heavily on the constant activity at the port, where containers filled with desperate souls were hidden among legitimate cargo.

The Vargas family kept their activities under the radar through connections in the shipping industry and law enforcement. Isabella employed a mix of intimidation and manipulation to ensure that port authorities turned a blind eye to her operations. Known for exploiting legal loopholes, she made it difficult for the police to gather sufficient evidence against her. Her influence extended deep into the community, with informants and loyalists positioned strategically to alert her of any impending threats. Isabella's charm and philanthropic facade, underscored by her sophisticated education and lavish lifestyle, masked the brutality of her operations, making her an enigmatic figure hard to pin down legally.

Head of the Delgado family, Carlos Delgado specialized in arms dealing and operated out of a remote warehouse in South Valley. Andrews examined a map of the area, noting the high security of Carlos's fortress-like warehouse. The Delgados' strength lay in their isolation and advanced surveillance systems. Carlos had transformed his warehouse into a fortress, complete with a private militia to protect his interests. The family dealt in a wide array of weapons, from small arms to sophisticated military-grade hardware, supplying various criminal organizations and insurgent groups.

Maintaining a low profile, Carlos avoided flashy displays of wealth and power that might draw attention. The Delgados conducted their transactions with utmost discretion, using encrypted communications and untraceable financial channels to stay ahead of law enforcement. Their operations were compartmentalized, ensuring that even if one segment was compromised, the rest remained intact. Carlos's ability to maintain tight security and operational secrecy made him a formidable opponent for law enforcement.

Despite the Foundry Hills Police Department's best efforts, apprehending these powerful criminal figures proved to be a daunting task. Corruption within law enforcement and other key institutions was a significant barrier. Hector Cartwright, Isabella Vargas, and Carlos Delgado each had allies within the police force and local government who provided protection in exchange for hefty bribes. This insider assistance allowed them to stay ahead of many investigations and raids that had been carried out in the past.

The families were shrouded in secrecy and protected in their criminal activities. Police often lacked concrete evidence to directly link them to their crimes. Low-level arrests were made, but the higher echelons remained insulated from prosecution. They were each skilled in exploiting the legal system, finding ways to avoid prosecution. Isabella Vargas, in particular, used her knowledge of shipping laws and regulations to shield her human trafficking operations from scrutiny. Witnesses and potential informants were often too afraid to come forward due to the violent reputations of these families. Intimidation tactics guaranteed that even when the police managed to gather evidence, securing reliable testimonies was a challenge.

Photographs of the three known leaders dominated the board in the detective's section of the department. Each face stared back with an air of impunity, symbols of the criminal empires they commanded. Additional blank spaces on the board mocked the department with many unsolved cases that continued to baffle them. Yet, a fourth space remained conspicuously empty—an elusive phantom, the rumored true puppet master, cloaked in shadows.

Detective Andrews, his hand resting thoughtfully on his chin, scrutinized the network of information sprawled before him. He knew the key lay in the details. Every fragment of data, no matter how trivial it appeared, could be the breakthrough they desperately needed. The crimson eclipse tattoo was a critical clue, but it raised more questions than answers. Nightshade had executed one of the most brutal attacks on someone not affiliated with the criminal enterprise. But why? The question festered in Andrews' mind, demanding to be answered.

Chapter 6: The Wake

The wake took place at a funeral home miles from Harper's house, drawing friends and neighbors into a painful circle of shared grief. Opposite the coffins, Harper, clad in a black tuxedo, stood frozen before the photos of Denise, Alice, and James Jr. Each picture captured a story, a frozen moment of happiness that now seemed almost cruel. One photo, his favorite, showed Denise on her birthday, laughing uncontrollably with cake smeared across her face. He had playfully dabbed frosting on her nose, only for her to retaliate with a handful to his face. That candid shot perfectly embodied her infectious spirit and their playful love.

As he continued to sift through more photos of Alice and James Jr., soft murmurs filled the room behind him, carrying kind words and shared memories. Despite the comforting conversations and the presence of those who deeply cared, a profound loneliness gnawed at him.

Melanie, Denise's friend, approached. Her eyes, red and swollen, mirrored the same pain gripping Harper's heart. She had babysat the kids countless times, her presence a comforting reminder of happier days when the kids would race to greet her.

"James," she began, her voice trembling, "I'm so sorry. They were such wonderful people. Denise was like a sister to me, and your kids... I loved them as if they were my own." She rested her hand on his shoulder, offering a small measure of comfort.

"Thank you, Melanie. They loved you too."

Melanie managed a weak smile. "I remember when Alice and I made such a mess baking cookies in your kitchen. She was about eight, so full of energy and curiosity. And James Jr... he would come out covered in chocolate, looking like a dancing cookie monster. And Denise... how I loved her. We would hang out and gossip while she braided my hair."

As Melanie spoke, her smile faded, replaced by a pained expression. She sighed heavily, shoulders slumping under the weight of her grief. Tears slid down her cheeks as she offered a soft apology and walked away.

Sam and Greg watched silently as Melanie passed, her sorrow palpable. They exchanged a glance, their own emotions reflected in each other's eyes. Slowly, they approached Harper, joining him before the photo display, taking a moment to absorb the memories captured in each picture.

"James, we know there's nothing we can say to make this better, but we want you to know we're here for you," Sam said, his voice thick with emotion. He looked directly at Harper, his eyes glistening. "Denise, Alice, James Jr... they will always be remembered."

Greg nodded, his eyes rimmed with red. "Harper, look around. These people, your family's friends, are here because of the love and kindness Denise, Alice, and James Jr. shared. Your family's warmth created bonds that will never be broken. We stand by you every step of the way," he added.

Sam placed a reassuring hand on Harper's shoulder, offering silent support.

Harper nodded, grateful for their presence. The room buzzed with hushed conversations and the soft sounds of weeping, creating an atmosphere heavy with shared sorrow. He appreciated his friends' presence, a comforting anchor in this sea of mourning. Each face reflected the impact his family had on their lives, a testament to the love and compassion Denise, Alice, and James Jr. had shared so freely.

A few moments later, Seraphin approached, his demeanor somber. He moved with quiet grace, his face set in a mask of respectful sadness.

"Harper, I am deeply sorry for your loss," he said. "Your family… this is an unimaginable tragedy."

Harper looked up, meeting Seraphin's gaze. "Thank you, Mr. Seraphin," he replied. "I appreciate your kindness."

"I've seen how much your family meant to you. If there's anything you need, please don't hesitate to reach out."

Harper nodded. "It means a lot. Thank you."

Seraphin's gaze turned thoughtful, his eyes momentarily distant. "Harper, you've done great work with us and your work in Artificial Intelligence (AI) has opened my eyes to new possibilities. The ability to gather and analyze information swiftly and efficiently... It's remarkable. I can't wait to see what you can do when you get back into the office."

Harper acknowledged the comment. "In times of adversity, innovative solutions often emerge."

"Agreed. We can use your expertise in AI to help pave the way, not just in cybersecurity but in various fields," Seraphin continued.

"Maybe. We just need to make sure it doesn't fall into the wrong hands," Harper replied with a faint smile.

Seraphin nodded, glancing towards the front of the room. "Looks like the priest is about to speak. I'll find my seat."

As the priest approached the microphone, Seraphin's words lingered, leaving a subtle impression that there was more beneath the surface. His comments planted a seed of curiosity within Harper, hinting at a broader vision yet to be fully revealed.

The wake continued, and it was time for Harper's speech.

"Thank you all for being here," he began, his voice shaking. "Denise, Alice, and James Jr. were my world."

Harper adjusted his glasses, took a deep breath to steady his emotions, his hand trembling slightly. "Each of you has had a profound impact on our lives. This gathering is proof that life can change in an instant, and it's in those fleeting moments we discover the true value of what we hold dear."

"Denise was more than my wife; she was my best friend. One night, before the kids were born, we decided to go on a spontaneous trip to the beach. A canopy of stars shined above us as we talked about our dreams with the waves lapping in the background. Each star resembled a promise we made—buying our first home, having children, growing old together. Our gray hairs would represent those dreams turned into memories, shared with our children and grandchildren. Denise was the mold that held our family together through strength and endless bliss."

His voice faltered. "Alice was like a ray of sunshine, perpetually filled with energy and curiosity. It wasn't my scene, but Alice loved it, so we went to a parent-daughter paint night. When it was time to reveal our canvases, we were astonished to find the same image—a vibrant sunset over an ocean with seagulls soaring in the distance. Our minds were perfectly synchronized."

"And James Jr... my bright young man," Harper continued with a fond smile tinged with sadness, "He had a heart of gold and a thirst for knowledge that reminded me of myself. Countless nights were spent playing video games, and Jr. always guided us to victory. Those evenings were my solace, and I hope they were his as well."

Harper's voice cracked. "My family's absence has left an irreplaceable void in my heart. Seeing all of you here today, remembering them, brings me some measure of comfort." He glanced around the room, eyes misty yet determined. "Even though they are gone, their memories and the love they shared will forever endure within my heart."

"I miss you dearly," Harper confessed softly, his gaze lingering on their photos. "But I know they're in a better place."

The room fell into a heavy silence, broken only by the subdued weeping of mourners. Harper stepped back, fighting to contain his emotions as the priest continued the ceremony. The priest's voice resonated through the room, offering the final prayers. "We ask for peace for these departed souls and strength for those who remain. Let us remember the love and joy they brought into our lives and the harmony in the memories we shared."

As the priest concluded, he invited the mourners to come forward, pay their respects, and offer their sympathies to Harper. One by one, people approached—some offering a comforting word, others a silent hug. Harper felt the weight of their sympathy but also the emptiness of his loss. As the formalities drew to a close, the grievers began to disperse, leaving behind whispered condolences and lingering sadness.

Harper lingered for a moment after the wake, staring at the photos of his family. "Please forgive me," he whispered, clutching an emerald pendant in his hand as tightly as the resentment within his soul.

***

Harper drove aimlessly through the city, lights blurring into a kaleidoscope of colors across the windshield. Places that once held meaning now rushed past as mere specters of their former selves.

After what felt like hours, he finally parked the car and stepped out into the brisk night air. The city lay in slumber, oblivious to his anguish, with only the glow of a solitary streetlamp hinting at life.

He walked several blocks, each step heavy with purpose, until he found himself in front of a small shop on the outskirts of Foundry Hills. The exterior was unassuming, with a faded sign above the door. Harper turned the handle and pushed the door open, the bell above it jingling softly.

Inside, racks adorned with tactical gear and camouflage clothing were layered with dust. The air was thick with the scent of gun oil and aged leather. Targets and spent casings littered the corners, adding to the sense of a place suspended in time, untouched by the outside world.

Behind the counter stood a grizzled man, his eye narrowing suspiciously as Harper approached. Jagged scars ran across the left side of his face, evidence of a brutal encounter. His left eye and arm were missing, a black patch covering his eye and the sleeve of his shirt pinned up like a pirate captain's. His store was his ship.

Another worker emerged from the back room, pausing at the doorway. "Luther, I'm heading out. See you tomorrow."

Luther gave a curt nod. "Okay."

Harper stared at the patch and empty sleeve. Luther caught his look, his gaze sharp and assessing. He said nothing, waiting for Harper to speak.

"I need a gun," Harper said nervously. His words hung in the air, heavy with the gravity of his request.

With a thick, guttural accent, Luther eyed him for a moment. "And I need an arm and an eye," he replied, his voice rough. "What kind of gun are you looking for?"

"Um... something compact and small."

"Well, that narrows it down." Luther gestured towards a selection of firearms in a secured display case behind the counter. The glass revealed an array of weapons arranged on velvet-lined shelves. Pistols and revolvers of various makes and models gleamed under the display lights. The shop's walls were lined with rifles and shotguns above racks of ammunition.

Harper's gaze followed Luther's gesture, taking in the assortment of deadly tools. Each one represented a step further down the path he had chosen, marked by sorrow and vengeance.

Luther watched him closely, his expression a mix of curiosity and wary anticipation. "What do you want it for? Competition shooting, self-defense?"

"For self-defense," Harper replied.

Luther raised an eyebrow, noticing the bruise and cut on Harper's head. "You look like you could use some firepower, but I don't see you needing it for defending," he remarked, his gaze lingering on Harper's injuries. "More like someone looking for trouble."

Harper said nothing, his silence speaking volumes.

"Alright. This one here," Luther said, retrieving a glossy black semi-automatic from the case. "It's a 9mm, similar to what the Foundry Hills Police Department uses. Reliable and easy to handle." He cleared the weapon and set the safety lever.

Luther placed the gun on the counter, turning it slightly for Harper to inspect. "This is a Glock 19. It has a polymer frame, making it lightweight and durable. The 9mm caliber is known for its manageable recoil and stopping power. The trigger pull is smooth, and the safety features are intuitive, perfect for someone who needs to react quickly under pressure."

Luther reached under the counter and produced a box of ammunition. "I'll also provide you with 15 standard full metal jacket rounds free of charge. They're reliable for practice and self-defense," he said, emphasizing the last words with a knowing look.

Harper weighed the gun in his hand, its presence both unsettling and strangely reassuring. As he held it, memories of his family flashed before his eyes—their smiles, their laughter, now replaced by cold reality. "I'll take it," he said firmly.

Luther nodded. "Good choice. I'll need to see some ID and run a background check before we continue with the sale."

Harper handed over his driver's license. The man studied it briefly before looking up. He noticed Harper looking at his arm again. "Crazy, isn't it? I lost my arm and eye, but before I did, I looked a bit like you do right now. A man on a mission," he said, his voice low and serious. "For me, it was vengeance. I was out hunting birds with my dog one day. After a couple of hours, it started to get dark, so we made our way back to the vehicle with a collection of dead birds. Before we could reach it, a bear showed up. Damn campers must have left food around and attracted it. My brave, stubborn dog faced off with the bear. I pulled up my rifle, but it was no use—I had already expended all my rounds for the hunt. Neither backed down, and after a couple of bites, the bear killed him before it ran off into the woods. I went after it, thinking I could make things right, get my revenge. My gun was loaded when I found the bear, but not without a cost."

"Ended up with this scar," Luther said, pointing to the deep gash on his face. "And lost my eye and arm in the process. That bear didn't care about my vendetta. Then I asked myself, was it worth it? You bet it was."

The weight of Luther's words sank into Harper's thoughts. "What I mean to say is, whatever you're scheming right now, think it through. Vengeance has a way of consuming you, making you lose more than you can afford. There might be alternative approaches, paths that don't lead to more pain. I'll be right back; it will take a couple of minutes to get this check done."

Harper's gaze remained fixed on the counter, his mind wrestling with the gun shop owner's advice.

The bell jingled as the front door swung open, and two men stumbled in, their raucous laughter filling the shop. One of them knocked over a display of targets, sending them crashing to the floor. The sudden noise made Harper flinch, his heart pounding as memories of that fateful night surged back—the shattering of glass, the screams, and the sight of his family's lifeless bodies on the living room floor.

"Hey! Watch where you're going!" Luther barked, his voice sharp.

"Relax, old man. It—was an accident. Hey! This guy has one arm, what happened, man?" one of the men slurred, swaying on his feet.

Luther's eyes narrowed. "Get out of my shop. Now."

The men laughed but didn't move. Luther stepped out from behind the counter, wielding a shotgun. "I said, get out!" he roared, pointing to the door.

"Whoa, easy, man. We're going..." The men staggered out, still laughing but more subdued.

Luther turned back to Harper. "Sorry about that. Let's get this finished."

Still shaken, Harper nodded, Luther's voice pulling him back to the present despite the haunting images lingering in his mind. He took a deep breath, trying to steady himself.

"Your check came back clear. How will you be paying?" Luther asked, returning the gun to Harper.

"Credit card," Harper replied, swiping it through the machine. As he accepted the receipt, Luther reached under the counter and pulled out a sturdy leather holster.

"Take this," Luther said, handing it to Harper. "It's on the house. You'll need it for carrying the gun safely. Let me show you how to use it."

Luther demonstrated how to fit the holster on his waistband, securing it firmly. "Now, when you draw, do it like this," he instructed, guiding Harper through the motions. "Make sure your finger stays off the trigger until you're ready to fire. And flip the safety lever like this."

Harper followed Luther's instructions, practicing the draw and safety maneuver a few times until he felt more confident.

"Good," Luther nodded approvingly. He then handed Harper a box of ammunition. "Let's load it."

Harper watched as Luther demonstrated, carefully sliding the bullets into the magazine and then inserting the magazine into the gun. Harper repeated the steps, feeling the weight and gravity of each motion.

"Take care of yourself," Luther said, his voice gruff but not unkind. "And remember to think about what I told you."

Nodding to Luther's advice, Harper walked back to his vehicle, the bell jingling softly behind him. Nearing his car, raised voices from a nearby alley caught his attention. The two drunk men from the shop had cornered a woman, bombarding her with crude and abusive comments.

He hesitated, but he couldn't just walk away. Steeling himself, he approached the men. "Hey! Leave her alone!" he shouted.

The men turned, surprise flickering into anger. One of them yanked out a knife, brandishing it with a twisted grin. The woman seized the moment, bolting away with rapid footsteps echoing as she disappeared from the alley.

"Great, you let her get away... we'll cut from you what you owe us," the knife-wielder sneered.

They lunged at Harper in unison. Harper dodged to the side, but not quickly enough. The knife slashed across his arm, a searing pain ripping through his flesh. The cut wasn't deep, but it was enough to send him over the edge. Blood oozed from the wound, dripping onto the pavement.

Instinctively, Harper's hand shot to his waistband. He drew the gun with a desperate urgency, the weight of the weapon both foreign and reassuring in his hand. The click of the safety disengaging echoed in the narrow alley. The men froze, their bravado draining away as they stared down the barrel of the gun.

Harper's voice, steady but seething with rage, cut through the tension. "All of you in Foundry Hills are the same—merciless, brutal, and heartless. I'd be doing the world a favor killing you."

The men glanced at each other, fear replacing their earlier drunken courage. In a sudden rush, they turned and bolted, their footsteps fading into the night. Harper lowered the gun, a wave of relief washing over him. Had they not fled, he wasn't sure if he could have pulled the trigger.

Luther's words hit him again, deeper this time. Vengeance and violence weren't paths he wanted to walk. Putting the gun away, he made his way back to his car, the weight of his decision settling heavily on his shoulders.

***

Warren Court no longer felt like a home Harper wanted to return to. Instead, he drove back to the heart of town and checked into a furnished hotel room. The building was luxurious and modern, with polished glass doors and a well-lit, elegant lobby. As he walked in, the manager, a well-dressed man in his forties, greeted him from behind a marble counter.

"Good evening, sir. How can I assist you?" the manager asked, his voice professional and courteous.

"I need a room," Harper replied, his voice steady but hollow. "I'll pay for the week."

"Of course," the manager said with a polite smile. "We have a few options available. Perhaps the King Suite?"

"That will work," Harper replied.

"Excellent choice, sir. Let's see, to arrange for this suite, the total will be $2,800."

"That's fine. Put it on my card," Harper said, handing over his credit card.

The manager nodded and swiped the card through the reader. After a moment, he handed the card back to Harper. "Here is your credit card. Everything is in order with the transaction. Your room is located on the 15th floor, room 1502. This is the keycard you will need to enter your room, and the elevator is just around the corner here," the manager said, pointing. His tone was warm and accommodating. "You'll find all the amenities you need, including high-speed internet and a state-of-the-art security system. Checkout is at noon. If you need anything, please don't hesitate to contact the front desk."

Harper nodded, taking the keycard. "Thank you."

"My pleasure, sir. Enjoy your stay," the manager replied.

Harper entered the elevator and pressed the button for the 15th floor. As he ascended, a brief moment of calm washed over him, knowing the room would offer him distance from the place he once called home.

Outside room 1502, he unlocked the door and stepped inside. The room was spacious and elegantly furnished, with a plush king-sized bed, a glass table, and a leather armchair. Recessed lighting and large windows offering a panoramic view of the city skyline created an inviting atmosphere. Harper set his bag down and took a deep breath, the clean air filling his lungs.

In the quiet luxury of the hotel room, Harper sat alone with the only light coming from the city outside. The cold, metallic surface of the pistol lay on the glass table before him. He reached out, running his fingers over the smooth metal. James Jr.'s ghost appeared by the table, his face filled with confusion and innocence.

"Dad, why do you have a gun?" James Jr. asked, his voice echoing with curiosity and fear.

Harper's heart ached at the sight of his son. He knelt, trying to reach out, but his hand passed through James Jr., the coldness of the hallucination biting at his skin. "I'm doing it for you," Harper whispered, his voice trembling. "To make them pay for what they did to you... to Alice, to Mom."

James Jr.'s expression turned to one of sorrowful understanding. His form began to shimmer and fade like a fragile dream. "Will it change anything?" he asked, his voice growing distant. "Will it bring us back?"

Harper blinked away the disorienting vision and forcing himself to focus. The intruders from that night would pay. He didn't want peace or forgiveness; it was a vow to ensure that their transgressions against his family were met with unrelenting revenge. This was for Denise, Alice, James Jr., and for the man he had been forced to become.

Chapter 7: The Funeral

The funeral took place on a bleak, drizzling afternoon at Foundry Hills Cemetery, a place where joy went to perish. The cemetery, with its solemn tombstones and orderly rows of departed souls, was a graveyard of dashed hopes and unfulfilled dreams. Denise, Alice, and James Jr. were laid to rest beneath the somber canopy of weeping willows, their branches hanging low, mirroring the weight of sorrow that gripped Harper's soul. The overcast sky wept in unison with the mourners, each raindrop a tear for the lives lost too soon.

As the priest delivered his solemn sermon, Harper struggled to focus amid the relentless patter of rain that muffled the clergyman's words. His gaze flitted from one coffin to the next, each one a painful reminder like splinters of glass tearing at his heart. All that was left of his family rested beneath the grandeur of marble, their names chiseled into the icy stone.

Sam, Greg, Melanie, and several other mourners huddled under black umbrellas, safe from the persistent rain. Their faces blurred through Harper's tear-filled eyes. He stood there, numb, barely registering the comforting hands on his shoulder or their prayers. Only the wet earth, freshly turned and covering the coffins that once held his world aloft, felt real. Each shovel of soil seemed to drive home the finality of his loss, sealing shut the chapter of his former life.

Clutching a damp, crumpled eulogy in his hand, Harper listened as the priest's gentle yet resolute voice cut through the fog of grief. "Today, we gather to mourn the passing of Denise, Alice, and James

Jr. Harper. A mother, daughter, and son taken from us far too soon, leaving behind a void that can never be filled. Yet, amidst our sorrow, we must find the strength to cherish the light they brought into our lives, the love they shared, and the memories that will forever reside in our hearts."

The priest paused, his eyes scanning the assembly huddled beneath a sea of umbrellas against the gray sky. "In times of loss, it is natural to seek answers, to grapple with the meaning of life and the inevitability of death. But even in our darkest moments, we must hold fast to hope."

Harper felt a bitter irony in the priest's words—hope and light felt like distant concepts in his current reality. His mind recoiled from the notion of dawn and light when all he saw was an endless abyss.

"There is an ancient belief that shadows are not mere absences of light, but entities unto themselves, waiting for their moment to emerge," the priest continued, his tone imparting a solemn warning. "In our grief, we must remain vigilant. Not all shadows are malevolent; some may guide and protect us, while others may seek to ensnare us further in darkness. It is our choices in these vulnerable moments that define our path forward." His words cut through Harper's bitterness, planting a seed of unease deep within him.

The priest's gaze seemed to pierce through Harper, as though he knew of the turmoil within, the festering desire for retribution. The priest's voice softened, and he spoke directly to Harper, "And now, let us listen to the words of a man who has known great love and profound loss. A man whose courage and resilience shine through in these darkest of days. Let us hear from Harper, who carries the weight of loneliness yet embodies the enduring power of love."

Harper hesitated, feeling the weight of every eye upon him, but he knew he had to honor their memory with his own words. Stepping up to the pulpit, he unfolded the crumpled pages of his eulogy, each word a testament to his love and loss.

"My dear Denise, Alice, and James Jr.," Harper began, his voice wavering slightly. "Today, I am reminded not just of our final moments together, but of the joy and laughter that defined our lives." He looked out at the somber faces before him.

"The last family photo we took at Rolling Peaks captured one of the happiest moments of our lives. It was one of the first times we all had genuine smiles, especially James Jr., who shared a joke he picked up at school. He said, 'Hey Mom and Dad, how do red peonies greet each other?... 'Hey bud, how's it blooming?'" Alice chimed in, giggling, 'Hey James Jr., a peony for your thoughts.' We all laughed, and the camera captured the best of us. Everything about our time together was beautiful."

"But today, as I stand before you, I feel a part of me slipping away with each of you. Pieces of my heart will be buried with you today." He paused, his throat tightening with emotion. Memories flooded his mind—of bedtime stories, of family hikes, of shared meals around the table. Each memory a cherished thread in the fabric of their lives together.

"May you find peace and remain in our hearts forever." With that, Harper gently laid the crumpled eulogy on the pulpit, the ink smudged against his skin. As he stepped away, he felt a sense of peace wash over him—a fleeting moment of clarity amidst the storm of his emotions. His family was gone, their bodies laid to rest in the cold ground.

Harper knelt beside each grave, placing a single white rose on his family's resting places. "I'll find them, I promise," he whispered into the mist-laden air. A dull ache throbbed in his head, unsettling but not too painful, passing through him and leaving him momentarily dizzy and disoriented.

As he stood to leave, his eyes scanned the cemetery, his heart heavy with grief and resolve. That's when he noticed a black SUV parked at the edge of the cemetery. It hadn't been there earlier. He watched as it drove away slowly, disappearing into the distance.

***

Following the next day, Harper drove down to the south side of town, arriving at a local shooting range. Outside the range, his hand trembled as he held a gun case. Harper collected himself before entering. He had never shot a gun before, always having avoided violence. The smell of gunpowder and the muffled sounds of gunfire greeted him as he walked in, a stark contrast to his usual environment.

The shooting range was a hive of activity, with people of all ages and backgrounds honing their skills. Harper approached the counter, paying for his spot number and targets. The clerk handed him a waiver and some ear protection, eyeing him curiously as he signed the paperwork.

Shots echoed inside the range. Harper placed his ear protection on and moved to his assigned lane. He took a deep breath, steadying himself. He raised the gun. His mind flashed back to the intruders who had shattered his world, and a surge of anger and determination coursed through him. He squeezed the trigger, the gun kicking back in his hand.

"Missed," Harper murmured. He fired again. "Another miss."

"You're not hitting the mark there, son," a gruff voice said, tinged with empathy. "Need some help?"

Harper looked at the man, his scars familiar. "Luther?"

Luther nodded. "I see you're new to this," he remarked, his tone gentle despite his rugged appearance. "How about we start with the basics?"

Harper nodded. "That would be great, thank you."

He listened intently as Luther demonstrated the proper stance, grip, and aiming techniques. Luther's instructions were clear and practical, focusing on control and precision.

"Take your time," Luther advised. "Focus on your breathing. Feel the gun like it's an extension of your arm."

Harper raised the gun and fired a round. The bullet struck the target.

"Not bad," Luther commented, adjusting Harper's stance slightly. "But you can do better."

Harper persisted, each shot bringing him closer to the mark. Luther's guidance was invaluable, refining Harper's technique with patience and expertise. With each round fired, his accuracy improved, the cluster of holes inching toward the bullseye.

As the session progressed, Harper's initial discomfort gave way to a growing proficiency. The target showed undeniable progress, yet an unsettling feeling gnawed at him. Each shot felt like a step further down a path he wasn't sure he wanted to follow.

After the lesson, Luther assisted Harper in cleaning the gun, his expression thoughtful as he observed Harper's quiet determination. With practiced hands, Luther wiped down the weapon, his movements deliberate and steady.

"You're a quick learner, Harper," Luther remarked, his voice low and measured. "But shooting is not just about hitting a target; it's about knowing what's behind it. Every shot you take can leave a mark—not just on you, but on others as well."

"Thanks, Luther, not just for the session but your words as well."

Luther nodded.

Harper left the range, driving back to his hotel. He reflected on the day's events as the scent of gunpowder lingered on his clothes. The man he used to be would never have envisioned himself in this position, preparing for a journey of retribution. The rapid improvement in his shooting skills was undeniable, yet it came with a realization—he could become adept at something he wasn't sure he wanted to pursue.

***

Later that day, Harper sat alone in his hotel room with the gun resting on the table in front of him. The steady hum of white noise from the television provided a semblance of sanity in his solitude. The room felt like a tomb, the silence heavy and oppressive.

A growl from his stomach broke the silence. He picked up the menu and scanned the options, his eyes settling on a cheeseburger and French fries—simple comfort food. He picked up the phone and dialed room service. After placing his order, Harper leaned back in his chair, his gaze inevitably returning to the weapon on the table.

He stared at the cold, metallic object, a symbol of both his grief and his desire for vengeance. Memories of conversations with Denise flooded his mind. He could hear her voice, clear and reassuring, "Your brain is your best weapon, Harp. Never forget that."

A short while later, there was a knock at the door. He opened it to find a hotel staff member with a covered tray.

"Your order, sir," the staff member said, placing the tray on the table.

"Thank you," Harper replied, tipping the staff member before closing the door.

He sat back down and lifted the cover, the sight of the cheeseburger making his mouth water. He took a moment to appreciate the simple pleasure of the meal before taking a bite. As he chewed, the television droned on in the background, an advertisement catching his attention: "Unlock the power of AI for advanced cybersecurity. Protect your data! Secure federal, state, and local systems with confidence…"

Harper's mind stirred with intrigue. AI for cybersecurity wasn't just about protection; it was a tool he could mold to his advantage. Images of algorithms and system vulnerabilities flashed vividly in his mind. He imagined exploiting these weaknesses, gaining access to classified information with a few keystrokes.

The prospect excited and unnerved him in equal measure. He knew he lacked the resources to execute such plans alone. Determination surged within him, overriding his doubts. A revelation hit him like a bolt of lightning—he could use technology, not just brute force, to achieve his goals. The gun seemed almost crude compared to the sophisticated power of technology.

Without hesitation, Harper stood up, abandoning his half-eaten meal. He grabbed his coat, his mind set on a mission. The nearest tech store beckoned—a place where tools awaited to turn his ambitions into reality.

Driving through the city streets, he passed the baseball stadium surrounded by buildings and structures. Nostalgia washed over him like a tidal wave. He remembered driving through here with Alice and James Jr. to watch the Foundry Hills Sprites play against La Villa Residentes. The first time had been for Alice's birthday, the car filled with excitement as the kids predicted the game's outcome.

He recalled parking in the crowded lot, the anticipation building as they walked towards the stadium entrance. The roar of the crowd and the taste of hot dogs and nachos lingered on their tongues—it all felt like another lifetime.

Harper arrived at a parking spot and turned off the engine outside Foundry Tech. The building towered over the surrounding stores. Through the expansive front windows, Harper glimpsed gleaming displays showcasing the latest in technology—laptops, high-definition monitors, and an array of smart home devices, all meticulously arranged to entice tech-savvy consumers.

The store's signage glowed a vibrant purple, reflecting off the windshields of parked vehicles. Harper observed the scene, noting the steady stream of customers entering and exiting, each seeking the next best gadget to enhance their digital lives.

Stepping inside, Harper was immediately met by a cheerful employee in a purple shirt, the store's brand color contrasting sharply with the white walls and minimalist decor. The employee's smile was bright and welcoming, designed to put customers at ease.

"Welcome to Foundry Tech! Is there anything I can help you find today?" the employee asked, genuinely eager to assist.

Harper glanced around, taking in the store's layout. Rows of neatly organized shelves and display tables stretched out before him, each section dedicated to different products. The latest smartphones and tablets were displayed prominently, their sleek designs and high-resolution screens catching the light. Further back, the computer section boasted an impressive array of desktops and laptops, while the gaming area showcased the newest consoles and accessories.

"Yes, could you point me to the camera section?" Harper replied, trying to maintain a casual demeanor while masking his urgency.

"Certainly! What kind of camera are you looking for? We have a wide range—from doorbell cameras for home security to high-end professional photography equipment. Anything specific?" the employee asked, their eyes bright with enthusiasm.

"Not sure yet. I'll browse for now," Harper said, concealing his true intentions despite having a clear plan in mind.

"In that case, sir, you'll find them between aisles 9 and 11, right by the desktop computers," the employee said, pointing in the direction with a practiced smile.

"Thanks," Harper muttered, grabbing a shopping cart and heading toward the indicated aisle.

"You're welcome," the employee called after him, the sound fading as Harper moved deeper into the store.

Among the shelves of cameras, Harper carefully considered each product. He needed equipment that could breach security systems, provide surveillance feeds, and create a hidden network where he could operate discreetly. He picked out several wireless transmitters, enabling remote access to live feeds via his mobile device or laptop.

In the electronics section, Harper selected a high-end laptop with a sleek design and a powerful processor, ideal for multitasking and handling complex operations without a hitch.

Next, he picked up several USB drives, crucial for loading software, bypassing security measures, and accessing encrypted files. He also added a mobile device to his cart for accessing networks and feeds while operating in public.

To ensure anonymity in his digital activities, Harper secured a subscription to a virtual private network (VPN), shielding his online movements from prying eyes and keeping his activities untraceable, especially when using the hotel's internet service.

Approaching the checkout counter, Harper was greeted by a chipper cashier wearing a bright purple Foundry Tech polo shirt. "Good evening! Looks like you've got quite a haul today," the cashier said, scanning the items with practiced efficiency.

"Yeah, I have a lot to set up," Harper replied, trying to sound casual.

The cashier nodded, their eyes lighting up as they scanned the high-end laptop. "This model here is top of the line. Excellent choice! And these cameras—very discreet. Are you setting up a home security system?"

Harper smiled faintly, not wanting to reveal too much. "Something like that."

The cashier continued scanning the items. "You really know what you're looking for. The wireless transmitters and USB drives are a great addition. You're going to have a pretty solid setup."

As the last item was scanned, the cashier suggested, "We have a rewards card that lets you accrue points usable as cash for future purchases. Can I help set you up with one today?"

"Sure, why not," Harper said.

"Great! I'll just need your address to set it up," the cashier said, typing on the computer.

Harper began to recite his old address, "113 Warren Court..." He paused, the weight of realization hitting him. Clearing his throat, he quickly adjusted. "Actually, can I provide the address later?"

The cashier looked up, slightly puzzled but nodded. "Of course, sir. You can update it anytime. Here's a temporary card for now. Your total comes to $5,247.89."

Harper's eyes widened slightly at the total, the amount momentarily staggering him. He took a deep breath, composing himself quickly. This equipment was essential, a necessary investment for what lay ahead. The unknown future loomed large, and in his mind, the cost seemed insignificant compared to what he stood to gain—or lose. "No problem," he said, handing over his credit card.

As the payment processed, the cashier glanced up with a friendly smile. "Is there anything else I can assist you with today?"

Harper shook his head. "No, that should cover it for now."

The cashier put the bags in the cart. "Thank you for shopping with us! Have a great evening."

"Thanks," Harper replied, wheeling the cart toward the exit.

Leaving the store, Harper felt content with the tools he had purchased. Now it was time to put them to use. As he loaded the equipment into his car, his mind raced with plans and contingencies.

Each piece of gear was a step closer to uncovering the truth and seeking the justice his family deserved.

Chapter 8: Information Gathering

Back in his room, Harper unpacked his equipment with methodical precision, each device meticulously configured and interconnected. The expansive desk transformed into a staging area, with a high-end laptop at its center, flanked by multiple monitors that glowed with potential. The room, once a sanctuary of luxury, now bristled with purpose.

Starting with the laptop, Harper optimized its powerful processor and advanced security features. Each connection was fortified with encrypted protocols, creating an impenetrable fortress of digital protection around his system. The high-definition monitors were meticulously aligned, providing a panoramic view of various feeds and data streams.

He moved on to the cameras, configuring each miniature device for maximum effectiveness. The installation would wait until he pinpointed optimal locations, but he tested the wireless transmitters, ensuring seamless integration with his network. Each step was executed with the precision of a surgeon, the equipment an extension of his will.

Leaning into the city's existing infrastructure—traffic cameras, Department of Transportation feeds, and public surveillance systems—Harper wove a web of surveillance. He tapped into these feeds using his expertise to bypass security measures and gain access to real-time data. Binary code, ones and zeros falling on the screen, danced in an intricate manipulation of data streams and camera feeds, creating a comprehensive surveillance grid.

Satisfied with the robustness of his security setup, Harper conducted several test hacks. Each attempt was repelled successfully, confirming the integrity of his defenses. With everything operational, he awaited the influx of intelligence.

Harper's gaze flicked across the monitors, each screen displaying a different angle of the city. He adjusted his headset, the low hum of voices and the clatter of footsteps filling his ears from the various feeds. No longer a victim in his mind, he scanned the screens with the focus of a hunter seeking prey. His jaw tightened, a silent nod to the specters of his loved ones that seemed to linger in the room.

The hotel room was bathed in the glow of the monitors, casting an eerie light across Harper's determined face. Silence encased the room, broken only by the occasional beep of an alert or the click of keys as Harper continued his work. Hours blurred without respite, the line between night and day dissolving in the haze of his efforts. He fought against sleep, his eyelids growing heavier until he finally succumbed to a fitful slumber.

A voice from one of the feeds jolted Harper awake. He reached for the mouse, clicking to refresh the highlighted feed on his screen—an unauthorized access point into the police station's phone system. Using a custom-built software exploit, he had infiltrated their VoIP (Voice over Internet Protocol) network. The screen flickered to life, displaying the station's call logs and live audio feeds. Detective Andrews' voice crackled through the speakers.

Harper adjusted the audio feed, tuning in just as Andrews was speaking. "...and that brings us to the latest updates on the case," Andrews said, his tone serious. Harper pictured him standing in the precinct's briefing room, a whiteboard covered in photos, maps, and handwritten notes behind him. Andrews recounted the gruesome details of the Harper family murders.

"The leaders of the Nightshade organization are our main suspects in this investigation," Andrews continued, the sound of shuffling papers and murmurs of agreement audible in the background. "We're dealing with powerful families, deeply entrenched in the city's criminal underworld. Their influence extends far and wide, and we believe they have a hand in numerous illegal activities."

Harper listened intently, his mind racing as he processed the information. He opened another window on his laptop, diving into the police database he had previously breached. The digital labyrinth of files and records spread out before him, each piece of data a potential clue. He sifted through the documents, cross-referencing names, dates, and locations, his eyes scanning for any mention of the crimson eclipse tattoo.

With each discovery, Harper's resolve grew stronger. He uncovered references to the tattoo in various reports—interviews with informants, surveillance photos, and intercepted communications. The tattoo was a symbol of allegiance and power within Nightshade's ranks, a badge of honor and fear marking its members as part of the inner circle.

The more he uncovered, the clearer the picture became. The Nightshade organization was an untouchable network of criminals, their activities shielded by layers of secrecy and corruption.

Harper's fingers flew across the keyboard, compiling the data into a comprehensive file. Understanding the structure and hierarchy of Nightshade was crucial to finding who was responsible for murdering his family. His quest had only just begun, and the tools at his disposal—the high-end laptop, the surveillance equipment, and his unparalleled skills as a cybersecurity analyst—would be the instruments of his retribution.

Every step he took from this point forward was meticulously planned. Each action calculated to bring him closer to the truth.

Harper discovered that only three members bore the distinctive eclipse tattoo and created a large board outlining the three families, the suspects in his wife and children's murders: Cartwright, the Vargas, and the Delgado families. Each leader controlled a distinct realm of illicit activities. Cartwright was involved in drug trafficking, Vargas in human trafficking, and Delgado in arms dealing. Understanding their operations was crucial to uncovering their vulnerabilities and finding an opportunity to strike.

Harper manipulated the underworld with keystrokes, invisible and untouchable. His laptop buzzed with encrypted communications, hacking attempts, and data transfers, each move being placed like pieces in a chess match, positioning him to checkmate Nightshade.

As the data reeled in, Harper opened a terminal window. Information on Hector Cartwright's, Isabella Vargas', and Carlos Delgado's operations started pouring in. Routes prioritized by routine and consistent movements mapped onto his satellite program, identifying their base of operations within the industrial district, docks, and South Valley. Warehouses, factories, and boathouses were strategically and intellectually selected, ideal for moving their products in and out, shielded from plain sight and police patrols. The detailed images and blueprints on his screen also highlighted various security measures: from warehouse door locking systems, camera feeds, and alarmed facilities to heavily guarded complexes.

More criminal traffic pointed to an organization named the White Dagger Triad (WDT). Although Harper did not have anything against them, he realized they might be useful in the future. Led by Jin Tao, the WDT operated out of Rolling Peaks. Although there weren't significant reports tying them to crimes until recently, Harper deduced they might be looking to expand their reach. With Nightshade controlling the majority of the city's crimes, there could be a mutual interest.

Focusing back on Nightshade, Harper had several systems ready on his laptop but still more to do on the ground. In just a few minutes, Harper loaded the data onto his phone and packed his equipment into a backpack, with the letters A.H. sewn onto it. After exiting the room, he locked the door behind him, activating the security system via his phone—a fail-safe designed to trigger a procedure to corrupt the files inside. If compromised, the program would render the files within the laptop and cloud useless, ensuring no evidence remained. Getting into his sedan, Harper drove toward the district.

***

Parking several blocks away, Harper proceeded on foot, utilizing the cover of darkness to conceal his movements. The new moon hid its face, casting the city in shadow. Delivery trucks rumbled by, shaking the ground and gravel. Using stealth through the shadows, Harper scouted potential camera locations, noting blind spots created by buildings and obstacles. He needed to get higher.

Less than 100 feet away, Harper spotted a utility pole and carefully climbed it, installing a camera at its peak adjacent to the light. Waiting for his phone to connect to the camera, he read the signs spread through the fence line: "No Trespassing" and "Authorized Personnel Only." The connection was successful, confirming the warehouse's location on his map. Before he could come down, he heard voices approaching, prompting Harper to stay perched on the elevated ground, heart pounding. The height kept him safe from the guards' view, gripping the pole tightly.

"Yeah, Hector mentioned the 'X-12' container arriving tomorrow night?"

"Absolutely. It's headed for warehouse 17, as usual."

The distant rustling of bushes caught Harper's attention, prompting him and the guards to turn sharply. Harper held his breath, remaining motionless, waiting for the guards to pass. They departed with flashlights in hand, moving towards the source of the sound, disappearing from Harper's view. Finally, he could safely lower himself.

Near the warehouse, Harper noted the heavy guard presence, with multiple sentries patrolling the perimeter. He needed to evade them. Spotting a nearby building with a commanding view of the warehouses, he swiftly climbed an escape ladder, ascending 25 feet. At the top, he mounted a camera with a clear shot facing the vehicle bay entrance. Below, he observed intense activity—trucks loading and unloading cargo, possibly concealing narcotics. Just as he prepared to depart, the sound of a door opening on the opposite side of the building caught his attention, flashlights illuminating the corner. Harper dashed to the ladder behind him, descending rapidly but slipping, his scream echoing as he tumbled into a dumpster with a resounding crash.

Staggering to his feet amid bags of trash, Harper heard urgent shouts from above. "Hold it right there!"

He scrambled out and pulled up his hood, bolting through the alleyway. Guards emerged from another door at ground level, yelling, "Stop!" Their flashlight beams swung wildly as they chased Harper, their heavy boots pounding on the pavement behind him. Harper's breath came in short, strident gasps as he pushed his sprint to the limit.

"Stop! Get him!" one guard shouted, their footsteps closing in.

Harper glanced right, then left, and veered into a narrow alley. Spotting a homeless man lying on the ground, he vaulted over him, skidding around the corner and taking the next right. The guards pursued, their footsteps closing in, their breath ragged and out of sync with Harper's rhythmic pace. He saw a chain-link fence ahead and scrambled up it, fingers slipping on the cold metal. Dropping to the other side, he hit the ground running, adrenaline fueling his desperate escape.

The guards weren't far behind, their flashlights bobbing as they scaled the fence. Harper darted into another alley, his eyes scanning for a way out. He spotted a fire escape and leaped up, pulling himself onto the first platform. The metal rattled loudly, betraying his position. He climbed higher, the guards shouting below him.

"There he is! Don't let him get away!" The guards' shouts echoed behind him as Harper reached the roof, the sprawling cityscape spread out below. He sprinted across the rooftop, mustering every ounce of strength. With a daring leap, he cleared the gap to the next building, landing hard and rolling to absorb the impact, briefly slowing his pace. The sound of the guards' footsteps halted momentarily, buying him precious seconds to widen the distance. Ignoring the burning ache in his muscles, Harper pressed on without relenting.

Spotting a fire escape, he descended rapidly, taking the rungs two at a time, his movements guided by pure instinct. Reaching the ground, he melted into the shadows, blending seamlessly into the darkness. Though he could still hear faint echoes of the guards searching, their voices grew distant.

Harper raced through three more blocks until he reached his car, where he paused, ensuring he hadn't been followed. Satisfied that there were no signs of pursuit, he drove to a parking spot about two miles from the warehouses. Pulling out his phone, he tested the video feeds from both cameras. They functioned perfectly, responding to his commands and displaying clear footage of the targeted areas.

Monitoring the second camera's feed, Harper overheard voices discussing, "Who was that guy and what was he doing here?"

"Probably another squatter. We'll need to check back regularly to keep them out."

Relief washed over Harper as he realized the cameras were in place and operational as planned. "Alright," he muttered to himself, refocusing on the next phase of his plan. "I just need to monitor the Cartwrights in the district and wait for actionable intel. I could probably look into the Vargas operation in the meantime."

***

Based on intelligence, Harper identified the Vargas family as the controllers of human trafficking operations centered around the port near Foundry Hills. He recalled a memory of Denise, Alice, and James Jr. enjoying the carnival at the docks, where they relished spinning rides and funnel cakes. The laughter and bright lights of the carnival now seemed infinitely distant compared to the illegal activities associated with the docks.

The ports were full of yachts, both simple and luxurious like the "Angling Spear" and "Mermaids Fortune" lining the piers, their opulent facades concealing darker purposes. Harper knew surveillance here would be challenging due to heightened security. As he surveyed the area, he thought of a great idea after seeing the wandering vagrants in the area—it would be a perfect cover in a place well-known for them.

Stopping at a nearby liquor store, Harper scanned shelves lined with various bottles of whiskey. He needed something cheap yet potent, with a strong, pungent aroma that could bolster his disguise. Settling on a brand recognized for its harsh, almost medicinal scent, its label faded and the bottle dusty, it seemed a perfect match for the persona he aimed to adopt. Approaching the counter, he encountered the cashier—a middle-aged man with graying hair and a wary expression. Harper's clean-cut appearance and determined demeanor contrasted sharply with the typical customer profile for this area, especially someone buying such a brand of whiskey. The cashier's gaze lingered on Harper's face, searching for any hint of deceit or trouble.

Harper responded casually, placing the bottle on the counter. The cashier's suspicious tone didn't go unnoticed as he scanned the whiskey, eyes fixed on Harper throughout the transaction. There was a moment of hesitation, a silent contemplation that lingered before the cashier completed the sale. Harper paid with cash, swiftly pocketing the bottle.

"Have a good night," the cashier muttered, skepticism tinging his voice. Harper nodded in acknowledgment, leaving the store without a backward glance. He made his way towards a small park near the docks, known as a gathering place for the city's homeless.

In a secluded spot behind some bushes, Harper took a swig of whiskey, feeling the burn in his throat adding authenticity to his guise. He roughened his appearance, pulling at his clothes and tearing holes in his already worn-out jeans and shirt. Spotting a discarded coat near a sleeping homeless person, he exchanged several bills for it, the stained and threadbare garment fitting perfectly for his disguise. After donning the coat, he scooped up dirt from the ground, smearing it on his face and hands, ensuring it settled into the grooves of his skin and under his nails.

Harper tousled his hair, making it appear matted and disheveled, and rubbed dirt into it to complete his transformation.

As Harper stumbled down the sidewalk, a couple passed by, the woman clutching her partner's arm tightly. "Let's go, honey, we don't want any trouble," she whispered, her eyes nervously darting towards Harper. They hurried along, tossing some money in his direction. Harper watched the bills flutter to the ground but left them untouched.

Satisfied with the effectiveness of his disguise, Harper observed how convincingly he resembled a downtrodden drifter. He blended seamlessly into the surroundings, his grimy appearance exuding a palpable sense of despair. In a fleeting moment, he hallucinated Denise standing before him, her eyes wide with disbelief. "Look at you, Harper," she uttered in sorrow. "How far you've fallen from the man you once were." The vision flickered and vanished, leaving Harper with a pang of sadness. He looked at his hands and thought about the couple that just passed him. Miserably, he took two swigs of whiskey, spilling some on his coat accidentally but fulfilling the illusion of heavy drinking. He staggered slightly as he walked, mimicking the unsteady gait of someone deeply inebriated.

Harper stationed himself at the port, meticulously observing the ebb and flow of traffic and cargo. The air was filled with the noise of cranes hoisting massive containers, the hum of forklifts, and the chatter of dockworkers shouting orders. Cargo ships, with their towering hulls, loomed over the docks, their decks bustling with activity. The salty tang of the sea mingled with the scent of diesel fuel and rusting metal.

To evade heightened security, Harper moved cautiously, seamlessly blending into the bustling port. His disguise was convincing—a hobbled gait, a bottle of whiskey in hand—ensuring he went unnoticed amidst security focused on more obvious threats.

Identifying strategic locations along the perimeter, Harper discreetly mounted cameras. He chose spots atop light posts where shadows concealed the small devices and behind crates to blend with the dock clutter. Each placement provided clear views of crucial areas, strategically avoiding detection using darkness and port obstructions like shipping containers and machinery to mask his movements.

Deeper into the port, Harper's cautious approach paid off as he slipped behind containers and machinery. Suddenly, he froze, witnessing men guiding blindfolded women towards a shipping container. Partially obscured by cranes and containers, the scene was nearly invisible to casual observers. Muffled cries of the women and harsh commands of the men pierced the industrial sounds, adding a chilling layer of horror to the port's constant din.

Harper climbed a nearby building, using a rusty fire escape to reach the roof. The climb was precarious, the metal creaking under his weight, but he moved with deliberate care. Selecting a spot near the roof's edge, he installed a camera on a ventilation duct, ensuring it was discreet yet offered a clear view below where the women were being led.

Securing the camera with industrial adhesive, Harper adjusted its angle remotely via his mobile device, fine-tuning the focus for optimal clarity. The live feed displayed crisp details—the men's faces, container numbers, and the women's distress. Harper ensured the camera securely transmitted to cloud storage, safeguarding the footage.

Satisfied with his surveillance setup, Harper began to retrace his steps when approaching footsteps and hushed voices interrupted the stillness. Taking another swig of whiskey, he let more spill on his shirt before collapsing near a container, feigning drunkenness and confusion. Lying on the cold, hard ground, he kept his breathing shallow to avoid drawing too much attention.

"What the, what are you doing here?" one of the port security officers demanded, wrinkling his nose at Harper's disheveled appearance.

Harper muttered incoherently, his slurred words and exaggerated movements selling his act. He swayed on his feet, eyes half-closed, and took another swig from the whiskey bottle, letting some of the liquid dribble down his chin.

"Disgusting," a Vargas henchman muttered, gesturing for the officer to remove Harper. "Get rid of him before Vargas sees him."

Rough hands seized Harper, hauling him to his feet with unnecessary force. They shoved him away from the docks, their grip tight and unyielding. Harper stumbled, deliberately exaggerating his fall and hitting the ground hard. The men's laughter echoed around him, mocking and cruel.

"Get out of here, you filthy drunk!" one of them jeered, kicking at the dirt near Harper's prone form.

Harper groaned, slowly pulling himself up. The men continued to laugh, their derision shielding his true purpose. Despite the pain and humiliation, Harper remained resilient. He couldn't afford to break his cover.

"Let's see if he can make it to the gate without falling over," another henchman joked, giving Harper a rough shove forward.

Harper staggered, nearly falling but managing to stay on his feet. The men's laughter grew louder as they followed him for a short distance, continuing their taunts. Each step was a struggle, but Harper kept moving, his eyes fixed on the ground to hide the intensity of his focus.

Eventually, the men lost interest and turned back to their posts, satisfied with their fun. Harper gathered himself and staggered off towards the park. He kept his head down, blending into the shadows until he was sure he was out of sight.

Reaching the relative safety of the park, Harper paused to catch his breath. His heart pounded with adrenaline, but he knew the disguise had worked. He had avoided suspicion and gathered crucial intel. Now, he just had to get back to his car without drawing any more attention.

As he walked, he wiped the dirt from his face and straightened his clothes as best he could, shaking off the encounter. His body ached from the rough treatment, but it was worth the pain.

Finally reaching his car, Harper checked the camera feed, relieved to see a clear view of the containers. The images showed the Vargas men moving about, unaware of the surveillance.

Driving home as the sun began to rise, Harper reflected on the long night. The docks had been a treacherous battleground, but his perseverance had paid off. The Delgados would have to wait until later—the final piece of his plan to unravel the Nightshade organization. The road was empty, the city just beginning to stir. Harper's thoughts were a jumble of strategies and memories, the adrenaline slowly fading as fatigue set in.

***

In the hotel's bath, Harper let the hot water swathe him, steam rising around him. He recalled bathing with Denise, their intimate moments by candlelight. The warmth of the water and the flicker of the candles brought a moment of peace in stark contrast to his current reality. The memories of Denise's laughter, the feel of her touch, and their whispered conversations filled him with a bittersweet longing.

Emerging from the bath, he dried off and settled on the couch, his muscles aching. His attention fixed on the monitors displaying feeds from the industrial district and the docks. The cameras he had placed earlier were transmitting clear, steady images. He watched the comings and goings of the port workers, noting any suspicious activity.

Exhausted, he eventually succumbed to sleep, the night passing without dreams, leaving him feeling empty upon waking. The monitors continued to display the silent, ongoing operations. The screen showed a slow trickle of early morning activity, the calm before another storm. Harper knew that as the day progressed, he would have to be ready for the next move against Delgado.

The next morning, Harper's focus shifted to Carlos Delgado, notorious for his arms dealing operations from a secluded warehouse on the outskirts of South Valley. This remote location offered ample cover for their illicit activities, shielded by limited network access and numerous dead spots—an environment Harper needed to survey firsthand. The Delgados were known for their brutality and tight security, making this task particularly challenging.

Waiting until sunset, Harper drove towards the outskirts of Foundry Hills. The Delgados' compound was fortified with a high fence and patrolled by vigilant guards. Parking safely on a nearby hilltop, he used the fading light to navigate through the overgrown brush. From his vantage point, Harper had a clear view of the Delgados' warehouse. He watched the entrance through binoculars, noting the patterns of the guards' patrols and the arrival of various vehicles. Unexpectedly, the world around him shifted. The warehouse melted away, replaced by the familiar sight of his living room. Alice and James were playing on the floor, their laughter filling the space.

"Come play with us Dad!" Alice called, her smile wide and inviting.

Harper's heart ached at the sight. He took a step towards them, reaching out, but the scene dissolved as quickly as it had appeared. He was back on the hilltop, the warehouse in view. Shaking off the hallucination, Harper refocused and approached on foot, using the cover of night.

Crawling beneath the fence, Harper maneuvered into the compound and found a strategic position in a tree overlooking the main entrance. The tree's dense foliage provided perfect cover. As he began installing a camera, he overheard a conversation between two men nearby. One spoke with authority, discussing plans for an imminent shipment.

"We need to ensure the delivery arrives smoothly. The buyers are high-profile; mistakes are not an option," the leader emphasized.

The gravity of the conversation intrigued Harper, who remained concealed, listening in until they retreated into the warehouse.

"We're expecting fifty assault rifles, a dozen RPGs, and plenty of ammunition. Warehouse 3 is prepped as per The Nightshade leader's instructions," the leader continued.

Frustratingly, Harper found the camera feed dead upon testing it multiple times. A potent communications disruptor in the vicinity rendered surveillance impossible without significant risk. Acknowledging defeat for now, Harper returned to the fence undetected and moved cautiously to his car.

On the drive back, Harper wondered about his next steps due to the failed surveillance. Upon reaching the hotel, he parked in the underground garage and made his way to his room. Testing the camera feed again from the safety of his hotel room confirmed its continued failure. The disruptor collocated near the compound was too effective. Pondering his next move, Harper reviewed the accumulating footage and notes on the Cartwrights, Vargas, and Delgados—each family's strengths, weaknesses, and operational details. The data was invaluable, painting a comprehensive picture of the Nightshade organization. Despite the anxiety from his close calls and haunting images of trafficked women, Harper pressed on with his mission.

Chapter 9: Hector Cartwright

Towering smokestacks and expansive factories in the industrial district fueled the city's relentless pursuit of growth. The operation of machines released chemical odors, polluting the air of Foundry Hills. It was here that Hector Cartwright's empire was built on the backs of countless workers producing the drugs that fed the city's dark underbelly.

At night, the district transformed into an abandoned landscape. The streets were deserted, save for the occasional figure scurrying into the darkness. This was Cartwright's domain, a place where the boundaries between legality and criminality blurred, and the line between life and death was razor-thin.

Hector's foray into drug smuggling began in his turbulent youth. Enduring brutal abuse from his alcoholic father, he escaped by joining the military, though his integration proved challenging due to lingering scars. Eventually, he gained recognition within the

Nightshade organization through a mix of intimidation and strategic alliances, earning the distinctive eclipse tattoo.

Beneath their veneer of wealth and influence lay a darker reality: the Cartwright Cartel orchestrated a symphony of crime from shadowy backrooms to opulent penthouses. They trafficked narcotics with the fluidity of water, their profits soaring alongside their expanding influence. Each transaction was a deceptive ballet, with Hector as the master choreographer.

Their success extended beyond the drug trade. They engaged in arms trafficking, money laundering, extortion, and racketeering. Their reach stretched into every dim recess of the city and beyond, a pervasive network ensnaring everything it touched.

Relentlessly pacing in his hotel room, Harper fixated on the screens before him. His small sanctuary had transformed into a war room, walls adorned with notes, photos, and diagrams mapping the intricate Cartwright empire.

He monitored Cartwright's enforcers and shipments for long hours, meticulously noting every detail.

Information streamed across one screen, revealing patterns in their movements. Surveillance footage scanned city feeds, identifying faces and vehicles with accuracy. A notification alerted Harper to Hector Cartwright's presence, sparking anticipation in the darkened room.

Electronics hummed, keys clacked, and muttered frustrations punctuated the air. Coffee cups and takeout boxes cluttered the desk—a testament to his singular focus. Harper had become a ghost in his own life, tethered only to this mission.

Beyond his window, neon downtown lights painted the night sky. Emergency vehicles streaked through the streets, their lights staining asphalt in red and blue. Distant sirens wailed—a constant reminder of the nearby chaos.

A camera near Cartwright's warehouse captured something unusual. Harper leaned closer, tension tightening in his chest. Hector Cartwright emerged with his entourage—an uncommon sight, as Hector typically shunned the limelight, delegating to underlings.

They moved decisively toward a freshly arrived freight truck. Streetlights cast elongated shadows, but details were discernible. The truck, marked "Vanguard Rentals," stood innocuously yet unsettled Harper.

In his notebook, Harper logged timestamps, packages, and faces. The scene unfolded with practiced precision—a criminal ballet. Harper delved into Vanguard Rentals' database, breaching security to extract crucial details.

Watching, a cold fury brewed within him. This enterprise wasn't just business—it was an empire forged on suffering. Each drug package symbolized shattered lives and fractured families. Hector Cartwright presided over it all, a man with an eclipse tattoo visible on his hand—a maestro of corruption.

The faces of Hector's men were hard and devoid of remorse. They were cogs in Cartwright's machine, potential weak points in his empire. Every empire had its cracks, and Harper was determined to exploit them. His mind raced with possibilities, strategies to dismantle the Cartwright operation piece by piece.

He envisioned the day when Cartwright's empire would crumble, reduced to rubble. The thought fueled his determination, pushing aside the exhaustion threatening to overwhelm him. Rest would have to wait until justice was served.

Night stretched on, the city outside his window unaware of the brewing conflict within its streets. Harper was prepared. Each day brought him closer to his goal. His war room, meticulously organized with evidence and maps, was more than an obsession; it was the nerve center of his crusade. He vowed not to cease until Hector Cartwright was dug into the ground.

***

At Foundry Hills Police Department, Detectives Andrews and Ramirez navigated through a chaotic scene outside the precinct. Protesters, incensed by the unchecked crimes of the Nightshade organization in Foundry Hills, clashed with officers at barricades. The air was thick with tension and shouts of frustration. Despite the turmoil, Andrews and Ramirez moved with purpose toward the entrance.

Approaching the door, Andrews exchanged a nod with the officer on duty. Inside, Andrews headed directly for the booking desk, his gaze fixed on the officer behind the counter.

"We need to question a suspect," Andrews stated, his voice cutting through the precinct clamor.

The officer looked up from his paperwork, assessing Andrews and Ramirez with guarded scrutiny. "Who?" he asked skeptically.

"Low-level guy with ties to the Cartwrights," Andrews stated flatly. "Josh, he's already in holding."

The officer acknowledged with a nod, gesturing for Andrews and Ramirez to follow him to the holding cells. Amid the chaotic room, the scratching of pens against paper marked their progress through necessary paperwork. Once done, they escorted Josh, the suspect, to the interrogation room.

Inside the observation room, Andrews and Ramirez huddled together as they strategized.

"We have to approach this strategically," Andrews began, his voice low yet commanding. "Can't afford to spook him before we get intel."

Ramirez nodded thoughtfully. "Agreed. Let's build rapport first. Ease into it."

They planned, debating questions to subtly extract information about the Cartwrights' operations. With a strategy set, they entered the interrogation room.

Josh sat at the table, eyes darting around. His fingers toyed with his jacket.

"Let's begin," Andrews said calmly, taking a seat opposite Josh. He placed photos of Harper's family and the crime scene on the table, sliding them toward Josh.

"What's this about?" Josh asked, his voice trembling slightly, trying to stall.

"We're discussing your involvement with the Cartwrights," Ramirez interjected firmly. "Tell us everything."

Josh's eyes widened with fear, but he remained silent, his lips pressed tightly together. He knew his lawyer was on the way and was determined not to betray the Cartwrights.

Andrews leaned forward, locking eyes with Josh. "Cooperate. It's your best option. Look at these pictures," he said, pointing to the photos. "Recognize them? This is Harper's family. They were murdered in cold blood by Nightshade. Those with the eclipse tattoo, we need to know which one of them did this."

Josh swallowed hard, his tension palpable, but he didn't utter a word.

Ramirez leaned in, his voice taking on a sharper edge. "You think staying silent is going to help you? We can make things a lot harder for you, Josh."

Josh's hands trembled slightly, but he kept his silence, eyes fixed on the table.

Andrews slammed his hand on the table, the sharp sound echoing in the small room. "Come on, Josh! You know something; names, locations—anything you can give us!"

Josh flinched at Andrews' outburst, fear evident in his wide eyes, yet he stayed silent, his loyalty to the Cartwrights unwavering.

"Think about your future," Ramirez pressed. "Is this loyalty really worth your freedom?"

Josh shifted uncomfortably, his silence a wall between them.

Frustration creased Andrews' brow deeply as he glanced at Ramirez. The interrogation had hit a dead end; Josh seemed genuinely loyal and too fearful to talk. With a resigned sigh, Andrews gestured to the observation room, signaling that their session with Josh was over.

Exiting the room, they were met by Josh's lawyer, Thomas Sanchez, whose smug grin greeted them like a challenge. "Well, well, well, if it isn't the dynamic duo," he taunted, his tone dripping with sarcasm. "What trouble have you boys gotten yourselves into this time?"

Ramirez stepped forward, his irritation simmering beneath the surface. "Cut the act, Sanchez. Your client isn't as innocent as you're trying to make him out to be. And if I can be frank, neither are you."

Sanchez chuckled dismissively. "Innocence is a matter for the courts, Detective. And from what I've seen, you're running on fumes here."

Andrews squared his shoulders, meeting Sanchez's gaze evenly. "We'll find what we need, one way or another."

Sanchez raised an eyebrow, his grin widening. "Sure, you can try. And remember boys, my client has rights, rights that can take that badge of yours if you're not careful."

With that parting shot, Sanchez turned and strolled away, leaving Andrews and Ramirez seething in his wake.

Andrews gritted his teeth, his fists tight at his sides as he stared down Sanchez. The lawyer, a known ally of Nightshade, was always ready to broker some shady deal. Andrews felt a surge of frustration and anger, knowing justice would continue to elude them as long as Sanchez remained in Nightshade's pocket.

Ignoring Sanchez's smug remarks, Andrews pushed past him. Sitting at his cluttered desk, he stared at the evidence board plastered with photos and documents related to the Cartwrights. Their smirking faces mocked him, fueling his anger.

***

In the lobby, Harper helped himself to a selection of evening snacks laid out on a table. He picked up a small plate and began to load it up with salami, pepperoni, and provolone cheese with some crackers. A presence beside him made him glance up.

"Hey there, never seen you around?" a woman's voice cut through the quiet ambiance.

Harper looked up to see a woman with cascading black wavy hair and sparkling brown eyes. Her natural charm stood out against her white skin. She wore a midnight blue evening dress, its modest neckline and classic cut complementing her approachable demeanor and warm smile, drawing others to her effortlessly.

"Yeah, checked in a couple days ago," he replied briefly, his attention divided between the woman and the food.

"Well then welcome, my name is Margaret," she said.

"Harper," he replied.

Margaret seemed undeterred by Harper's curt response, launching into a friendly interrogation about his stay. Her eyes dropped to his hands noticing a wedding band, engraved with the initials J & D.

Her eyes raised back towards Harper's. "So, how are you and the family settling in? This place can be a bit overwhelming at first with all the traffic, but it's got its charm. Lots of great things to do here."

Harper gave vague answers, eager to return to the solitude of his hotel room and the tasks awaiting him. "We are doing fine, I mean, I'm still getting used to this place, and my family will not be joining me here. Hopefully, I can join them soon."

Margaret's enthusiasm didn't wane. "Ah, I understand, on business then I assume? Well, either way, this place takes some getting used to. It even took me some time to adjust, what with all the noises and residents and whatnot. Look at me, chatting away with a plate full of food. I hope you settle in quickly and join your family soon. Um, Harper, right?" She extended her hand, her French-tipped nails adding a subtle sophistication to her gesture.

Harper forced a polite smile and shook her hand. "Yes, that's correct Margaret, and thanks. I hope so too."

Margaret walked away with a graceful stride, her movements exuding an effortless elegance that captivated those around her.

Making his way back upstairs and entering his room, Harper placed the plate of cheese and meats beside the laptop. He went to the refrigerator and grabbed a carbonated water.

Seated at his desk, he powered up his laptop, his fingers over the keyboard like a maestro playing a grand piano. Bypassing Vanguard Rentals' security protocols posed a challenge he welcomed. With meticulous care, he targeted system vulnerabilities, skillfully navigating firewalls and decrypting protected files. The AI and machine learning algorithms he had deployed tirelessly sifted through data, extracting crucial information.

He took a bite of cheese and a cracker as more data filled his screen—shipment logs, employee records, financial transactions—all pieces of a complex puzzle. Harper took a gulp of the water, studying the uncovered evidence revealing Vanguard Rentals' unwitting involvement in cartel activities. Their trucks had been used to transport illicit goods disguised as legitimate cargo.

His surveillance feeds in the Industrial District provided vital insights. Harper focused on a warehouse, meticulously reviewing its layout. He discovered remote-controlled doors and an elaborate camera and audio system connected to the warehouse office—a perfect setup for his plans.

Now, Harper needed a strategy to lure Hector into the warehouse trap. With the information from Vanguard Rentals' system, Harper understood how the Cartwright Cartel disguised illegal shipments within supposed legitimate goods, like machinery parts and agricultural supplies. After taking a sip of water, he released sophisticated algorithms to scour dark web forums, decrypt encrypted chats, and analyze external surveillance footage. All data pointed back to Hector Cartwright and Nightshade, painting a detailed portrait of the cartel's clandestine activities.

Discovering a vulnerability in the cartel's software, Harper exploited a backdoor overlooked by their supposed security experts. Through this access, he tracked a shipment of high-grade heroin scheduled to arrive at one of the cartel's usual warehouses in the industrial district. The timing was predictable—late at night when the streets lay quiet and law enforcement turned a blind eye.

But from the logs, Harper could see that Hector was not always present at these deliveries. To ensure Hector's presence during the shipment's arrival, he planted false information using one of the cartel's communication networks. Hacking into a secure account, he crafted a message suggesting a newly formed gang, the White Dagger Triad (WDT), had learned of the shipment and planned an interception. The message was succinct yet potent: "We have information of a shipment that will be arriving at Warehouse 17 in the Industrial District tonight. Get ready to intercept. – Jin Tao."

From previous sources, Harper knew that Jin Tao and his organization wanted to expand their reach. This was their opportunity. Using an anonymous, encrypted messaging system he had developed, he reached out to the WDT, posing as a traitor from within the Cartwright Cartel. He provided them with detailed information about the shipment, including its location and scheduled time. His message to Jin Tao, their leader, was direct: "Cartwright and a large drug shipment, tonight in the Industrial District, Warehouse 17, 3 a.m."

The promise of high-grade heroin was enough to pique their interest, but shortly after, Harper received a skeptical response: "Who is this and why should I believe you?"

Harper, prepared for this, replied with a screenshot of the logs from Vanguard Rentals, showing the arrival details of the rental van. He also attached previous footage of them unloading at Warehouse 17 from the Vanguard Rentals van. "Here's your proof. Cartwright's operation is real, and tonight's shipment will be your only chance to strike, taking down Hector and beginning your reign over Foundry Hills."

The compelling evidence was sent, and Harper could tell from the increased communication activity on devices linking back to the triad that they were mobilizing for the interception. However, Jin Tao's cryptic response left Harper uncertain if he had fully convinced him. Only time would tell if Jin Tao and the White Dagger Triad would show.

With both factions now set on a collision course, Harper settled into surveillance mode in his hotel room. Remote cameras monitored the scene outside, transmitting feeds to his device. The night air was thick with tension, a palpable sense of impending conflict hanging in the silence.

CHAPTER 10: CARTWRIGHT'S FATE

Harper took another sip from his beverage, a ring of water marking where he had picked it up from. He quickly wiped it down and improvised a coaster to prevent it from wetting the table further. Minutes passed as he monitored the feeds, his eyes scanning every detail. Glancing at his watch, Harper felt adrenaline surge through him as the appointed time approached.

The monitors showed a live feed from outside Warehouse 17, capturing the arrival of the anticipated convoy. Six black SUVs pulled up in front of the warehouse, their headlights slicing through the darkness like searchlights in a prison yard. Facial recognition software automatically identified Hector Cartwright as the man who emerged from the third vehicle. Armed enforcers flanked him, submachine guns at the ready, forming a shield of ammunition against any potential threat.

"Secure the area! Eyes on every corner!" Hector's authoritative voice rang out, amplified by the tension coursing through him. Harper noticed the specific radio frequencies being used by Hector and his men displayed on his monitoring screen. Using the intelligence he had gathered beforehand, he hacked into these frequencies, gaining access to their encrypted channels, capturing every directive and response exchanged among them. The enforcers spread out around the warehouse, vigilant and poised to repel any perceived threat, casting a foreboding shadow over the scene.

Harper's pulse quickened as he activated the audio feed from the surveillance cameras, tuning into the live transmissions from inside the warehouse. Hector's gruff voice pierced through the static, commanding his troops with his nervousness apparent, betraying cracks in his facade of confidence.

From his command center in the hotel room, Harper monitored every move Hector made. He queued up a soft melody on the warehouse's audio system, a subtle lure amidst the surveillance feeds. Moments later, Hector's head tilted slightly as the faint strains of music reached his ears. Suspicion flared in his eyes as he followed the sound.

The heavy metal door of Warehouse 17 groaned open, revealing Hector cautiously stepping inside, his automatic submachine gun held at the ready. He scanned the dimly lit interior, alert for any sign of danger. Just as the door closed behind him, Harper remotely activated the locking mechanisms on all entrances, trapping Hector inside.

Inside the warehouse, Hector glanced back at the doors, assuming they had simply settled shut. Suddenly, Harper's voice boomed through the warehouse's PA system, echoing eerily across the vast space. The unexpected sound startled Hector, causing him to whirl around, searching for the source.

"Hector Cartwright," Harper's voice resonated.

"Who's there?" Hector barked, his voice thick with forced confidence, masking his unease.

"I am your unfinished business," Harper growled, his tone crackling with rage. "You took something from me. You and the others murdered my family. Each of you will pay. But before you do, I demand to know why." Each word was a bullet, loaded with vengeance and the agony of loss.

Hector sneered, his pride flaring as he touched the bulge on his head. "It's you? You left me this hideous mark. I'm going to find you and kill you, I don't care what they said about keeping you alive," he snarled, firing a burst of gunfire into the shadows, the rounds' impacts echoing off the walls.

"Unfortunately for you, you'll never get the chance. Before the next 30 minutes are up, you'll be just another statistic in Foundry Hills," Harper said.

"Your words are meaningless, I'll call my men; they will find you," Hector said.

In the tense silence that followed, Harper typed furiously, sending a fabricated message over the warehouse's audio system in Hector's own voice.

"Foundry Hills police, this is Hector Cartwright. I have information on Nightshade and the murders they carried out. I would like to make a deal in exchange for protection and immunity," the voice proclaimed, eerily authentic in its replication of Hector's gravelly tone.

Panic flashed across Hector's face as he realized the gravity of Harper's manipulation. "What? How did you— That's not me!" His desperate protest was cut short by the realization of Harper's leverage.

"You still think my words are meaningless? How you die will be determined by the information you give or don't give me. I can make your associates hear exactly what I want them to hear, and they'll treat you like they do with traitors. I'm sure you know that fate well. Or, you tell me what I want to hear, and I'll do you a favor, a quick death."

"I was there but I didn't kill anyone. It was Carlos Delgado. He ordered us to go, just to scare the family, nothing more," Hector stammered, his voice betraying his desperation. "If I refused, I would have lost my standing within Nightshade." His admission hung in the air, a damning revelation that exposed the inner workings of the cartel.

In that moment, Harper knew he had struck a critical blow. The dominos were falling, and Hector Cartwright's reign of terror was unraveling one confession at a time.

"Why should I believe you? You need to give me more," Harper demanded.

Hector moved towards the exit, his hand grasping for the door handle, only to find it locked, defying his futile attempts at escape.

"Damn it!" Hector cursed, desperation tainting his voice as he rattled the door with increasing urgency. His once-confident demeanor crumbled, replaced by a primal instinct for survival as he realized the gravity of his predicament.

But it was too late. The electronic locks held firm, confining him within the warehouse like a trapped animal. Panic surged through Hector's veins, cold realization settling over him like a suffocating shroud. With every futile tug at the unyielding door, he confronted the inescapable truth: there was no way out.

He turned around, his voice rising in defiance. "Because it's the truth!" Hector shouted. "Look, I have proof." He fumbled with his phone, swiping the screen repeatedly. Finally, he displayed a series of text messages, holding it cautiously, unsure if anyone was watching. Spotting a camera, Hector marched towards it, raising his phone. "See!"

Though obscured from Harper's view through the surveillance cameras, a quick hack into Hector's phone revealed an incoming message stating, "I know the hit was unusual for us, but it had to be done." The subsequent message read, "Mr. S was more than satisfied with our execution." The messages were cryptic, avoiding explicit names but hinting at a higher authority.

Harper remained silent, scrutinizing the messages from Hector's phone with a keen eye. "You and your cartel flood Foundry Hills with drugs, ruining lives, escalating crimes, resulting in the deaths of innocent people."

Hector's voice faltered. "I'm just doing what I must to survive. I can give you information you want. I'll tell you everything." He hesitated, then added urgently, "Do you want to know about Carlos Delgado? I can tell you everything, just let me go."

Harper observed, his expression inscrutable as he watched Hector texting frantically on his phone, unaware that Harper had already infiltrated his communications. Hector attempted to send a message: "I'm trapped, Warehouse 17."

"They can't help you, Hector," Harper said coolly. He revealed that he had traced the message to Leo, a member of Hector's cartel waiting outside the warehouse. "Leo and the others won't be able to use their phones now, and neither can you. I have control over all devices traced back to your network. Tell me about Carlos."

Hector exhaled shakily. "Carlos Delgado handles the arms shipments. He's the distributor within Nightshade. But getting to him is impossible. South Valley is heavily guarded; there's no way you could reach him from inside."

"Where can I find Delgado outside of South Valley and his fortress?" Harper asked, his tone devoid of emotion.

"He has a taste for going out to one of the clubs after work, not sure when but I know he does it often," Hector replied, his voice strained with urgency. "These clubs are unique, where women aren't the usual entertainment."

Harper absorbed the information quickly, planning his next moves around Carlos Delgado's routine. But first, he had to finish what he started with Hector Cartwright.

"Thank you for the information," Harper said calmly, his expression remaining unreadable.

Hector's relief was short-lived as Harper's tone turned colder. "It's time, the final hour has come for you to face the consequences of your crimes."

Hector made another attempt to exit through the locked doors, frustration evident in his movements. He glanced towards the surveillance cameras, where he could feel Harper looking back at him. Outside, Hector's men could be heard clamoring urgently, their voices carrying through the thick warehouse walls.

"What's happening in there, boss? Why isn't the door opening?" one of them shouted.

"Keep trying, damn it! Get me out of here!" Hector yelled back, his voice tinged with desperation.

Undeterred by the commotion outside, Harper remained focused. With a few keystrokes on his laptop, he sent a final encrypted message to the White Dagger Triad's (WDT) network. The message: "Hector Cartwright is yours." Through his surveillance cameras, he watched as shadows moved stealthily on the exterior of the warehouse, their movements masked by the cover of night. It was the WDT.

Recognition software picked up Jin Tao emerging from the shadows. WDT's leader stood out with a silver sash, taking charge of the operation. His team strategically placed explosives throughout the warehouse. Harper observed the details unfold with thorough clarity, noting the operatives' precise actions and deliberate movements as they unpacked materials from their bags.

As the operatives completed their setup, Harper watched with a grim sense of determination. The warehouse, once a stronghold for Hector Cartwright's cartel and one of Nightshade's sources of power, was now on the brink of destruction—a fitting end to Hector's reign of crime and terror.

A truck carrying the shipment of drugs rolled into the warehouse lot, its arrival perfectly timed with Harper's intel and the WDT's meticulously planned ambush. As Hector Cartwright's men cautiously approached the vehicle, anticipating an intercept but unaware of the Triad's precise tactics, they were suddenly engulfed in a storm of gunfire. WDT operatives, positioned strategically on elevated positions surrounding the warehouse, opened fire. The hail of bullets created chaos and confusion among Cartwright's enforcers, who were outnumbered and caught off guard by the unexpected assault. Triad members launched distractions—smoke grenades and flashbangs—further disorienting the cartel's men and disrupting their ability to coordinate a defense. Amidst the chaos, Cartwright's enforcers struggled to react effectively, their numbers swiftly dwindling under the relentless assault.

Inside his hotel room, Harper intently monitored the unfolding chaos. The flickers of gunfire and the shouts of commands streamed through the surveillance feeds, painting a vivid picture of the violent showdown outside the warehouse. Each scene captured the brutal reality of Hector's criminal enterprise unraveling in real-time—a testament to the Triad's overwhelming firepower and strategic advantage.

Trapped within the warehouse, Hector's panicked voice crackled through the audio feed. "What's happening out there?" he demanded, his tone laced with fear and confusion.

"The White Dagger Triad, they're everywhere!" shouted one of his men.

Harper responded coolly. "They're here for your shipment, Hector. And soon, they'll be coming for you."

Hector's desperation escalated. "Please, I can pay you—money, drugs, anything you want! Just let me go!"

Watching Hector's distress on the monitors, Harper remained unmoved by the cartel leader's pleas. "Your time is up, Hector," he stated flatly, his voice devoid of sympathy.

Outside, Jin Tao, the Triad's leader, signaled for the final phase of their operation. Explosions ripped through the warehouse, shaking its foundations and sending flames roaring into the night sky. Harper remotely unlocked the warehouse doors, granting Jin Tao access to Hector.

Through the billowing smoke and flickering flames, Jin Tao confronted Hector with chilling calmness. "Your reign in the drug trade ends tonight, Hector," he declared, his voice carrying an air of finality. "The White Dagger Triad will ensure you and your empire are nothing but a memory."

Defiant to the end, Hector sneered. "You think you can stop us? I'll kill you all!" He raised his rifle and opened fire, the shots echoing through the warehouse. Jin Tao swiftly dove behind a stack of crates, avoiding the barrage of bullets.

Hector's shots rang out with a deafening intensity, the muzzle flash illuminating his face twisted with rage. The acrid smell of gunpowder filled the air as he emptied his magazine, the bullets ricocheting off metal surfaces and tearing through wooden crates. Jin Tao peeked from his cover, his eyes locked onto Hector's frenzied movements.

With a snarl, Hector tossed his empty rifle aside, the clatter of metal against concrete marking his urgency. He reached beneath his coat, fingers fumbling for the grip of a secondary pistol. His hands shook with adrenaline as he pulled the weapon free.

Jin Tao seized the moment. With a burst of speed, he lunged from behind the crates, his movements a blur. The dagger in his hand glinted ominously as he closed the distance between them. Hector's eyes widened in surprise, the pistol only half-drawn when Jin Tao's blade sliced through the air.

The dagger found its mark, cutting deep into Hector's arm. Blood sprayed from the wound, the bright red droplets spattering the ground like rose petals scattered by the wind. Hector roared in pain and anger, clutching at his arm. "Pathetic. A little scratch. You are dead!" he spat, but his voice wavered with uncertainty.

He attempted to raise the gun, his finger curling around the trigger, but his body betrayed him. A numbness spread from the wound, creeping up his arm and into his chest. His legs buckled, and he collapsed to his knees, the gun slipping from his grasp. He stared at his trembling hands, disbelief etched across his features.

"This is the end for you, Hector," Jin Tao whispered ominously, his voice echoing through the crumbling warehouse. He stepped back, watching as the realization dawned on Hector's face.

Hector's eyes widened in terror. "What... what have you done to me?" he choked out, fear deep in his voice. He tried to move, but his limbs felt like lead, heavy and unresponsive.

Jin Tao paused, his gaze piercing yet serene. "This is the essence of Aconitum whitei," he explained calmly. "Found in my home within Rolling Peaks. Do you feel it? Its poison traveling through your body, paralyzing you, keeping your body separate from your mind. Consider it an honor—a worthy end for those who cross the path of the White Dagger Triad."

Hector's breath quickened, panic setting in as he comprehended the gravity of his situation. "No... you can't..."

"You'll stay here and witness the rise of the White Dagger Triad," Jin Tao said quietly, his voice carrying an air of inevitability. He turned away, leaving Hector to confront his fate amidst the echoes of collapsing walls and fading footsteps.

Outside, the Triad swiftly secured the drug shipment and eliminated the remaining cartel members, leaving no trace of Hector's criminal network behind. Harper watched from his monitors, his expression grim as he witnessed the fiery demise of Hector Cartwright's empire. The warehouse became a blazing inferno, consuming everything within its walls—including Hector, trapped and powerless in his final moments. Amidst the crackling flames, Hector's screams echoed, a desperate cry lost in the infernal roar.

As the flames danced in the night sky and smoke billowed, Harper knew Hector had met his deserved end. With the White Dagger Triad vanishing into the darkness, leaving the warehouse ablaze, Harper turned from the monitors. The screens flickered and then went dark, overwhelmed by the destruction outside. Methodically, Harper severed all connections to the warehouse, ensuring no digital traces remained. Amidst the chaos, a cold satisfaction settled over him, knowing one of those responsible for his shattered world was gone. Now, his sights were set on his next target: Carlos Delgado.

Harper shut down the computer systems and rose from his chair, stretching his tired muscles. Just minutes ago, the room had been filled with the clamor of destruction, but now, only silence remained.

Delgado remained elusive and difficult to approach. Yet, Harper's background in ethical hacking had honed his ability to uncover hidden vulnerabilities. He pulled up a detailed map of the city on his laptop, concentrating on the warehouses scattered throughout South Valley. Gathering intelligence on Delgado's movements, habits, and connections would be crucial, requiring patience and further planning.

***

Harper ventured into the cool night air, making his way to his car. As he started the engine and drove towards the outskirts, he received an alert of a voicemail pending on his phone. Disregarding it for now, he tuned into the local radio station. The announcer's voice crackled through the speakers, urgent and grave.

"We have breaking news," the announcer said. "Explosions and a fire have erupted in a cluster of warehouses located within the Industrial District. Police are en route, and we will keep you updated as this situation develops."

Harper listened intently, a grim satisfaction settling over him. He knew the chaos he had left behind would divert attention and attract more police chatter in pursuit of Nightshade.

Arriving in South Valley, Harper parked his car in a secluded spot, quietly observing the activities around the warehouse complex. The valley stretched out before him, a desolate expanse of land dotted with warehouses that stood like silent sentinels against the night sky. Workers moved about, handling cargo under the crescent moon, accompanied only by the occasional passing train. Carlos Delgado's operations were centralized in one particular warehouse, its fortified structure giving it the appearance of a military installation rather than a place of commerce.

Harper scanned the area, searching for any sign of Delgado or his associates. The radio continued to provide updates in the background, each mention of the fire reinforcing the success of his earlier operation.

"Authorities have cordoned the area and are investigating the cause of the blaze," the announcer reported. "Initial reports suggest it may be connected to recent criminal activities in the region."

A figure emerged from the darkness—a man whose authoritative presence stood out among the workers. Despite the obscured features, Harper discerned the confident demeanor and the subtle deference shown by others. This was likely Carlos Delgado, the man he sought. He watched the man suspected of being Delgado using binoculars from his vehicle. Delgado navigated paths between crates and containers with familiarity, reinforcing Harper's suspicion that he was no ordinary warehouse employee.

Delgado entered a secluded warehouse away from prying eyes. Harper, unable to breach the heavily guarded perimeter fences, mentally mapped out potential scenarios. He considered the best ways to exploit Delgado's routines and the layout of the warehouse complex, noting possible entry and exit points and areas of weak security. Harper found himself stymied by the patrols on the perimeter and was unable to make any further progress for the time being.

Driving through the streets back to his hotel, he couldn't shake the haunting memory of Hector's agonized cries playing on a loop in his mind. The pursuit of justice was exacting its toll, pushing him to the edge. Hallucinations seized him. In the darkness of the car, Denise, Alice, and James Jr. appeared as spectral forms, flickering before him like phantoms. Startled, Harper swerved, narrowly avoiding a collision with another vehicle. The blaring horn and screech of tires snapped him back to reality, his heart racing as he struggled to regain his composure. The vividness of the hallucination left him shaken.

Gripped by disbelief and grief, he pressed on, determined to channel his pain into action. Upon reaching his hotel room, Harper sought refuge from the haunting memories that tormented him. With trembling hands, he poured himself a shot of whiskey, the amber liquid offering a temporary escape. As it burned down his throat, it did little to quell the storm of emotions raging inside him.

In the solitude of his hotel room, Harper approached the wall where Hector Cartwright's photo hung, his fingers curling into fists. With a surge of resentment and anger, he tore down the photo, feeling a bitter taste in his mouth as he did so. Without hesitation, he tore it in half and tossed it in the trash.

Chapter 11: Industrial District's Massacre

As morning light filtered through the overcast sky, Detective Andrews arrived at the scene of Hector Cartwright's demise. Warehouse 17, now reduced to a charred skeleton, exuded a potent mix of smoke, burnt debris, and lingering dampness from the previous night's rain. Firefighters persisted in extinguishing the remnants of the blaze, their headlamps piercing through the haze with focused determination. Approaching the lead investigator, Detective Trevors, Andrews took in the scene—a battlefield of ash and twisted metal punctuated by the acrid scent of scorched debris. Trevors, appearing weary but focused, met Andrews with a grim expression.

"What have we got?" Andrews inquired, his voice edged with concern.

"A massacre," Trevors replied solemnly, gesturing towards the wreckage. "All of them are Cartwright's men. The fire was deliberate, explosives were used—precise and controlled. It was a professional hit."

Andrews studied the ruins, his mind sifting through potential motives and suspects. "Any witnesses? Anyone who might have seen something?"

Trevors shook his head. "Nothing yet. This area is quiet at night. If someone saw or heard anything, they haven't come forward."

Andrews entered the warehouse and shifted his gaze to where Hector's charred remains had been discovered, marked by a somber barrier of police tape. Gathering himself, he stepped outside in front of the warehouse, the squelch of mud underfoot mingling with the crackle of dying embers.

"Any leads on who could have pulled this off?" Andrews asked, his eyes fixed on the grim scene.

Trevors sighed heavily. "No. But whoever did this wanted to send a message. This wasn't just about eliminating Hector—it was about making a statement. Could be another syndicate trying to muscle in on Cartwright's territory."

Straightening up, Andrews issued orders to Trevors. "Get forensics in here. I want every inch of this place combed through. I need to know what kind of explosives were used, how they were triggered, and any traces of the attackers we can find."

Trevors nodded, already relaying the directives to his team. Andrews turned away, scanning the debris-strewn ground for any clues. He felt a sense of familiarity in the attack—the precision, the custom-made munitions hinted at a calculated assailant, one with resources and intent.

A forensic officer interrupted his thoughts, presenting a bullet casing. "Detective, take a look at this," the officer said, handing over the casing. "These markings—they're not standard. Looks custom-made."

Examining the casing closely, Andrews recognized the intricate engravings along its base. "I've seen these before," he murmured, reading the letters on the brass, "WDT."

The analyst nodded solemnly. "We've uncovered something that might be significant, Detective Andrews."

Andrews nodded in acknowledgment as he approached the makeshift workstation set up on the hood of a police car. The scene around him buzzed with activity—officers combing through debris, firefighters still battling hot spots, and the lingering smell of smoke and charred wood.

The analyst gestured to the screen of a laptop hooked up to various forensic tools. "We've been analyzing the surveillance footage from the surrounding area. Most of it was destroyed in the explosion, but we managed to salvage fragments."

Andrews leaned closer, his eyes fixed on the grainy images playing on the screen. Despite the damage, enough remained to piece together a narrative of the night's events. Shadows moved in and out of view, vehicles approaching under cover of darkness, and figures wearing masks and tactical gear.

"We isolated this sequence," the analyst continued, zooming in on a particular frame. "This vehicle arrived shortly before the attack. It matches the description of a black SUV we've been tracking in connection to other criminal activities."

Andrews studied the footage intently. The SUV was nondescript, blending into the urban landscape effortlessly. Yet, its presence at the scene of the crime was a glaring clue.

"Do we have a plate?" Andrews asked, his voice taut with anticipation.

The analyst shook his head. "No plates."

"Keep digging," Andrews ordered, his mind racing with possibilities. "I want to know where that vehicle came from, who was driving, and where it went after the attack."

The analyst nodded, already tapping away at the keyboard to enhance the footage and run facial recognition algorithms. As Andrews watched, a knot of tension tightened in his stomach. The puzzle pieces were beginning to fit together—the custom ammunition, the precision of the attack, and now, a potential lead with the black SUV. But he knew there were still gaps to fill, loose ends to tie. Turning away from the laptop, Andrews surveyed the warehouse ruins once more. The devastation was profound, a stark reminder of the violence that had erupted here. He paced the perimeter, his footsteps crunching on broken glass and charred debris, his mind processing the unfolding information.

"Detective Andrews!" an analyst called out, breaking through his thoughts. It was Emily Berg, approaching with a sense of urgency, tablet in hand.

"What have you found?" Andrews asked, turning to face her.

Berg handed over the tablet, displaying a series of updated images and notes. "I dug deeper into the ammunition markings," she explained. "It looks like these rounds are linked to a recent series of arms deals involving a group known as the White Dagger Triad. They're a small but ambitious group operating out of the city outskirts."

Andrews nodded thoughtfully. "The White Dagger Triad," he murmured. "I remember them now, but how could they pull off such an attack?"

"It gets more interesting," Berg continued, scrolling through her findings. "There's chatter about their leader, Jin Tao, attempting to expand the WDT's influence. If they're behind this, it aligns with a motive of making bold moves to establish dominance."

Andrews took in the information, his mind racing through the implications. "Find out everything you can about them," he instructed. "Their leadership, their operations, any recent movements. I want to know who we're dealing with."

Berg nodded, already engrossed in her tablet. "I'll get right on it, Detective."

As she walked away, Andrews turned back to the warehouse. The investigation was far from over, but with each piece of evidence uncovered, he felt closer to unraveling the mystery. The White

Dagger Triad—a new player in Foundry Hill's criminal underworld, ruthless and ambitious. They had made their mark, but Andrews was determined to ensure it wouldn't go unanswered.

Andrews stood in the rain-soaked streets, his coat pulled tightly around him against the cold and dampness. He had spent hours at the warehouse site, sifting through debris and evidence, trying to make sense of the brutal attack that had claimed Hector Cartwright's life. The forensic team had uncovered crucial leads—custom ammunition, a mysterious SUV seen before the explosion, and now, a trace of a sophisticated cyber intrusion into the warehouse's security system.

"We found a trace of an anomaly in the warehouse's security system logs," Berg explained, pointing to her laptop screen. "It looks like someone hacked into the system just before the explosions. They covered their tracks well, but we managed to find a small data signature that doesn't match any known cybercriminal groups."

Andrews leaned in, studying the data with furrowed brows. "Can we trace it?"

Berg shook her head regretfully. "We tried, but it's like a loop that keeps resetting. They were meticulous. Almost no trace left behind, and what we did find is incredibly difficult to follow."

"Keep at it," Andrews instructed firmly. "This might be our only lead."

Andrews departed the scene and headed downtown. The rain fell harder as he navigated through the crowded streets, his thoughts consumed by the case. Lost in contemplation, he accidentally bumped into a passing pedestrian.

"Sorry," muttered the man, barely glancing at Andrews before continuing on his way.

Andrews paused, turning to watch the stranger disappear into the throng. There was something oddly familiar about him—the way he adjusted his glasses, his brief and hurried demeanor. The letters "A" and "H" embroidered on his backpack stirred a sense of déjà vu in Andrews.

Shaking his head to clear his thoughts, Andrews resumed his journey. He couldn't afford distractions, not now. But the encounter lingered in his mind, leaving an unsettling feeling that there was more to it.

***

Thomas Sanchez stepped into the nightclub, the pulsating beat of electronic music reverberating through his bones. The club was packed with men, some engaged in hushed conversations while others watched attentively as a male dancer performed on stage. Sanchez took note of the absence of women, a subtle indicator about Carlos Delgado's personal preferences.

Delgado sat in a corner booth, surrounded by his men. His eyes locked onto Sanchez the moment he entered. With a nod from Delgado, one of his bodyguards waved Sanchez over.

"The great attorney Sanchez," Delgado greeted him with a cold smile, his eyes glinting with curiosity. "What do you have for me?"

Taking a deep breath, Sanchez steadied his voice. "Delgado, Hector Cartwright and his men have been murdered. There were no survivors."

A flicker of anger crossed Delgado's face, his jaw tightening. "Hector's dead?"

"Yes," Sanchez confirmed, his heart pounding. "I overheard some men at the department. They believe the White Dagger Triad is behind it."

Delgado's eyes narrowed further, and he leaned back, a dangerous calm settling over him. "The White Dagger Triad," he repeated slowly. "So, they think they can move against the Nightshade?"

The tension in the room was palpable. "You better have more than just suspicions, Sanchez," Delgado said, his voice dripping with menace. "I need solid intel. Whoever did this will pay dearly. I'll personally see to it that they are put through the fabricator."

Sanchez's stomach churned, but he forced himself to stand tall. "I'll find out more from the department and bring it back to you."

Delgado's expression turned even more menacing, and he grabbed Sanchez's arm, yanking him close. "Don't fail me, Sanchez. Or I'll put you through the fabricator as well."

The sudden movement sent a jolt of fear through Sanchez, and he felt his knees weaken. The men around Delgado watched with predatory interest, waiting for their leader's next move.

"I won't fail you," Sanchez managed to say, his voice trembling slightly. "I'll get the information."

Delgado released him with a shove, and Sanchez stumbled back, nearly losing his footing. "You better," Delgado snarled, his eyes boring into Sanchez's.

Sanchez nodded, his heart racing as he backed away. He turned and quickly made his way out of the nightclub, the cold night air hitting him like a slap. Once he reached his car, he couldn't hold it in any longer. He let out a scream of frustration and anguish, pounding the steering wheel with his fists. Tears streamed down his face as the weight of his situation crushed him. He was tired of the constant threats, tired of working for Nightshade, and desperate for a way out.

As he sat in his car, the reality of his predicament settled over him like a heavy cloak. He needed to find a way to survive, to break free from the clutches of Nightshade. But for now, all he could do was drive away and hope that he could gather the information Delgado demanded before it was too late.

***

Harper sat before his computer screens, monitoring surveillance feeds from the cameras he had strategically placed around the city. The rain drummed against the window, casting a melancholic rhythm to the air. He was focused on his mission: to uncover the truth behind his family's murder and exact vengeance upon Carlos Delgado.

In the background, classical music played softly from the radio, blending with the patter of raindrops. A commercial interrupted his focus, "Coming back to Foundry Hills at the Theater of Performing Arts, Romance in the Gardens starring John Lathom and Tori Wakowski," followed by a nostalgic tune from a Broadway musical.

Harper's mind drifted momentarily to happier times—standing in line with Denise as they awaited entry to "Romance in the Gardens." The memory of their shared anticipation, their smiles filled with love and hope, briefly warmed his heart amidst the cold reality of his current existence. But the fleeting reminiscence quickly gave way to the starkness of his present reality. The memory of finding Denise's lifeless body, surrounded by shell casings, and the devastating discovery of Alice and James Jr. in the closet flooded his mind. The pain and anguish were as raw as ever, a reminder of why he had embarked on this relentless quest for justice.

Pushing aside the haunting memories, Harper refocused on his task. He delved deeper into his research on Delgado and Vargas, meticulously reviewing footage and gathering intel on their operations. His determination burned fiercely, fueled by caffeine and sheer willpower as he pieced together every detail that could lead him closer to his target. His eyes were bloodshot, the result of countless sleepless nights spent scouring information and plotting his next move.

The phone rang, jarring him from his thoughts. He glanced at the caller ID and saw Sam's name flashing on the screen.

"Hey, Sam," Harper answered, his voice rough with fatigue.

"Harper, it's good to hear your voice," Sam replied warmly. "Listen, I know things have been... rough lately. I was thinking, why don't we grab lunch today? It might be good to catch up on things."

Harper hesitated, glancing around his cluttered hotel room. The thought of stepping outside, of being around people, was daunting. But Sam's concern was genuine, and Harper knew he couldn't keep isolating himself forever.

"Alright, how about the 5th Street café? I can meet you there in an hour," Harper said, trying to muster enthusiasm.

"That sounds great," Sam agreed. "I'll meet you there."

"Okay," Harper ended the call and took a deep breath, steeling himself for the social interaction ahead. He knew Sam was trying to help, and maybe a change of scenery would do him some good.

An hour later, Harper sat across from Sam at the corner café, where the faint aroma of freshly baked bread and sizzling bacon wafted through the air. The cozy ambiance was punctuated by the chatter of patrons and the clinking of cutlery against plates. Despite the pleasant surroundings, Harper's eyes were heavy with exhaustion, dark circles etched beneath them. His fingers drummed absently on the table as he waited for the waitress to arrive.

Sam observed Harper with a furrowed brow. "Harper, you look like you haven't slept in days," he remarked gently, his voice laced with sympathy. "How are you holding up?"

Harper offered a half-hearted shrug, his gaze drifting to the window where pedestrians rushed by, oblivious to the turmoil churning within him. "I'm managing," he replied, his voice rough with weariness. "Just taking it one day at a time."

The waitress approached, her notepad in hand and a warm smile on her face. "What can I get for you gentlemen today?" she asked cheerfully.

"I'll have a turkey sandwich," Harper said, forcing a smile as he handed her the menu.

"And for you?" she asked, turning to Sam.

"I'll have the club sandwich," Sam replied, his attention never straying far from Harper.

As the waitress moved to the next table, Harper's ears picked up snippets of a conversation between a nearby family. The father was ordering for his young daughter, who sat eagerly at the edge of her seat. "Could we get the pizza with extra olives, please? She just loves them."

Harper's heart tightened at the mention of extra olives. A vivid memory flashed before him: Alice, his sweet daughter, her face lighting up with delight as she ate her side order of olives, a request she always made at restaurants. "Oh, how she loved them," he murmured under his breath.

The warmth of the memory was quickly overshadowed by the cold reality of his present. His family was gone, ripped away from him by the cruelty of fate and the hands of those he now hunted. The sandwiches arrived, the scent of roasted turkey and crisp vegetables mingling in the air. Harper took a bite, the flavors bursting on his tongue, but the food felt like ash in his mouth. His appetite had long been lost to grief and vengeance.

Sam watched Harper chew mechanically, his concern deepening. "Harper, you don't have to do this alone. There are people who care about you, who want to help."

Harper swallowed hard, setting his sandwich down. "I appreciate it, Sam, but this is something I have to see through. For them."

Sam sighed, leaning back in the booth. "Just promise me you'll be careful. You're all that's left of them. Don't let their memory drive you to a place you can't come back from."

Harper nodded, Sam's words settling heavily on his shoulders. He took another bite of his sandwich, the flavors blending into a bitter reminder of the life he had lost. He resolved to stay vigilant and focused, knowing that every step he took brought him closer to justice, but also further from the man he used to be.

CHAPTER 12: DETECTIVE ANDREWS

Detective Andrews reclined in his chair, his gaze fixed on the sprawling crime board that dominated the dimly lit room. Frowning with intense concentration, he meticulously traced the lines connecting various pieces of evidence related to the Cartwright massacre. A recent breakthrough had linked shell casings found at the scene to the White Dagger Triad, a notorious criminal syndicate led by the enigmatic Jin Tao. Their ominous influence was expanding like a creeping shadow over the city.

Pushing away from his desk, Andrews strode purposefully through the precinct corridors. He exchanged nods with fellow officers in their crisp uniforms, the fluorescent lights overhead casting stark reflections along sterile white walls adorned with official portraits and building layouts. The distant murmur of coffee-fueled conversations drifted from the break room as he made his way towards the analyst floor.

Emily Berg, the department's esteemed analyst, sat engrossed in her work as Andrews approached her desk. Her unwavering focus softened only slightly as she looked up, meeting Andrews' determined gaze with her own. Her workspace bore witness to her dedication, cluttered with accolades like the "Analyst of the Year" award and meticulously organized case files marked with colorful tabs.

"Got a minute, Berg?" Andrews inquired, his tone a blend of urgency and curiosity.

"Sure thing, Detective," Berg replied calmly. "You're here about the Cartwright massacre?"

"Yes, any updates?" Andrews asked eagerly, leaning in.

Berg nodded, pulling out a folder labeled "WDT Brief" and handing it to him. "Ballistics confirmed our suspicions on the WDT. I've compiled everything we have on the Triad so far. Profiles of key players, including Jin Tao, and details on their weapons and ammunition are all there."

Opening the folder, Andrews studied its contents. Mugshots of Triad members stared back at him, alongside images of confiscated weaponry marked with the distinctive "WDT" engraving—a macabre trademark of their lethal craftsmanship.

"Good work, Berg. This is exactly what we need," Andrews remarked, his voice reflecting both gratitude and the weight of the task ahead.

"Thank you, Detective," Berg replied, her tone measured. "There have still not been any updates on the hacking incident, but I'll keep monitoring."

"Great, thanks again Berg," Andrews said, nodding appreciatively.

Returning to the investigations floor, Andrews gathered his team around the crime board. With deliberate motions, he pinned up the newly acquired photos, each face a potential link in the chain they sought to unravel. The board now painted a vivid mosaic of faces, locations, and timelines—a complex tapestry that demanded clarity and insight.

"Alright, team, listen up," Andrews began, his voice cutting through the charged atmosphere of the room. "We've established a connection to the White Dagger Triad."

Andrews sat at the head of the briefing room table, his team gathered around him in tense anticipation. Berg's meticulous analysis had linked the shell casings found at the Cartwright massacre to the White Dagger Triad (WDT), a revelation met with murmurs of concern and apprehension among his investigators. Lionel, a seasoned member of his team, voiced doubt.

"The WDT wouldn't risk something like this," Lionel interjected. "They're small-time players, not known for such brazen acts."

Andrews shook his head, his expression grave. "We have concrete evidence, Lionel. Their influence has been growing steadily. This was a statement."

"Why target the Cartwrights, though?" another detective queried, breaking the uneasy silence that followed.

"Good question," Andrews replied, rubbing his temples wearily. "We recently arrested a man who claims he delivered the vehicle just moments before the massacre. He was apprehended last night during a routine traffic stop, high on heroin."

"The driver?" Lionel raised an eyebrow, intrigued.

"Yeah," Andrews continued. "He was working for Vanguard Rentals, making frequent deliveries to the Industrial District. They paid him and others in heroin to keep quiet. We've struck a deal for his cooperation, hoping he can shed light on the cartel's operations."

Unease rippled through the room as Andrews addressed his team. The motive behind the attack was becoming clearer, yet deeper mysteries arose. He turned to the crime board, pinning up a photo marked with a question mark.

"Not just the WDT," he explained, gesturing at the board. "There's a third party involved, capable of sophisticated hacking. They breached the warehouse's security system, gaining control over the doors, audio, and video feeds. Our tech team found traces but couldn't pinpoint the source."

He tossed the logs onto the table, frustration evident in his movements.

"Bottom line, we need answers, and we need them fast," Andrews declared, his gaze sweeping over his team. "Dig into the WDT. Find their connections, their motives. And track down whoever this mystery hacker is. They might hold the key to Cartwright's killer."

As his team dispersed to follow their assignments, Andrews remained at the table, staring at the engraved shell casings. Despite their efforts, the case seemed to slip further from their grasp. He sighed heavily, the weight of unanswered questions pressing on his shoulders.

***

Andrews retreated for the evening to his sparsely decorated bachelor apartment. The living room was functional and minimalistic, featuring a black couch facing a large high-definition LED TV mounted on the wall. In one corner stood a treadmill, hinting at his disciplined physical routine. Passing his desk cluttered with case files and photos, his mind still immersed in the enigma of the WDT.

Moving to a small wet bar, he poured himself a drink—a nightly ritual to unwind after long days at the precinct. The scent of bourbon entered his nostrils as he took a contemplative sip. Sparse paintings adorned the walls, though few, hinting at a taste for art amidst the practicality of his surroundings.

At his home desk, Andrews picked up a photo of Jin Tao, leader of the WDT, studying the face that represented danger and mystery. Andrews recalled Jin Tao's backstory—a tale of a man who forged an empire from humble beginnings. Jin's father had immigrated to the country from Korea, with little but determination, building a small import-export business. Together, they had expanded into more illicit activities, turning their enterprise into a formidable criminal organization.

As he set the glass down, Andrews knew that unraveling the truth behind the Cartwright massacre would require unraveling the truth about the WDT and their intentions.

***

Harper focused intently on the surveillance footage, scrutinizing Carlos Delgado's weekly visits to a city nightclub. Each frame was analyzed as if it held the key to unraveling the mystery. Harper had dedicated countless hours to studying the tapes, observing patterns and routines. Delgado's punctuality stood out—he always arrived at the club after 11:45 PM.

As Harper watched the video, he observed the silver electric car approaching the warehouse gate, its headlights cutting through the darkness. He paused the footage and zoomed in, trying to glean a clearer view. Against the gritty backdrop of South Valley, the car's polished exterior stood out. Harper's brow wrinkled in concentration as he enhanced the image, fixating on the driver's side window. The camera captured Delgado's bald head and goatee clearly as he rolled down the window to speak with the security guard.

Delgado's calm and composed demeanor during these interactions suggested a man who felt secure in his power and control over the area. Harper noted the specifics of the vehicle—the make, model, and any distinguishing features. The car was a recent model, a silver electric vehicle that stood out amidst the worn-out surroundings of South Valley warehouses. The decision to use such a vehicle was intriguing; silent, efficient, and environmentally friendly, it seemed an ironic choice for someone involved in nefarious activities. However, Harper knew that modern electric vehicles relied heavily on advanced technology for operation and tracking, offering a unique opportunity to gather crucial information.

Harper decided to delve deeper into the vehicle itself, opting to conduct thorough online research. He navigated to the ElecVe dealership website, renowned for its selection of high-end electric cars. Scrolling through the listings, he compared the features and specifications with those resembling Delgado's model.

These vehicles were equipped with sophisticated GPS systems, onboard computers, and a plethora of sensors. This technological infrastructure could provide a wealth of data, potentially revealing Delgado's movements and routines. More intriguingly, Harper considered that accessing this information might also grant him the ability to manipulate the vehicle itself. His mind raced with the possibilities, realizing this could be his way in.

Focusing on the specific model, Harper delved into forums and technical documentation, learning about the vehicle's capabilities. He discovered that the car's software updates, maintenance records, and even its real-time location could be accessed with the right tools and knowledge. This insight was a goldmine; if he could hack into the car's systems, he could track Delgado's every move.

Harper needed more concrete information, so visiting the ElecVe dealership became imperative. Armed with this new lead, he knew he had to follow up in person. Gathering his notes, he prepared to leave his hotel room. This discovery was too significant to ignore; he was determined to uncover more about Delgado's activities.

As Harper exited his building, he encountered Margaret, who had just returned from a run, her earphones still in and sweat glistening on her face.

"Hey, Harper!" Margaret called out, catching her breath. "How's it going?"

"Hey, Margaret," Harper replied, nodding in acknowledgment. "Not bad, on my way out."

"Good to hear," Margaret said with a smile. "Oh, I have something for you. Hold on."

She disappeared briefly into her hotel room down the hall and returned with a freshly baked loaf of banana bread, still warm. "I made an extra loaf this morning. Thought you might enjoy it," she said, handing it to Harper.

He accepted it gratefully, feeling the warmth through the wrapping. "Thanks, Margaret. This looks amazing."

Margaret smiled warmly. "You're welcome! Hope you enjoy it."

Harper nodded appreciatively, holding the loaf in his hands.

As Harper turned to leave, Margaret's curiosity got the better of her. "Hey, Harper, can I ask you something?"

He paused, turning back to face her. "Sure, what is it?"

Margaret hesitated for a moment, then decided to go for it. "I noticed you're very quiet. Are you okay? I don't mean to pry, but you seem like you're carrying a lot."

Harper's expression tightened slightly, and he looked away, avoiding her gaze. "It's... complicated. Just dealing with some personal stuff."

Margaret nodded, her eyes filled with understanding. "I get it. Life can be tough sometimes. If you ever want to talk or just need a distraction, I'm here. I know we don't know each other well, but sometimes it helps to have someone to listen."

Harper forced a small smile, appreciating her concern. "Thanks, Margaret. I appreciate it. Maybe I'll take you up on that sometime."

Margaret smiled back, a hint of relief in her eyes. "Anytime, Harper. Take care."

As Harper walked away, he couldn't help but feel a small sense of comfort from the encounter. Margaret's kindness was a rare light. He wasn't ready to share his burden yet, but knowing someone cared made a difference.

***

Harper strode purposefully towards his car, a loaf of freshly baked bread tucked under his arm. As he navigated the bustling city streets, he passed by familiar landmarks and quaint cafes, his mind briefly drifting to the rare luxury of home-cooked meals amidst the blur of fast food and microwaved dinners that dominated his recent days.

Outside the sleek facade of the ElecVe dealership, Harper settled into the driver's seat of his parked car. Margaret's gift, a loaf of warm bread, beckoned to him. He tore off a piece, the familiar scent of Denise's homemade treats filling the car, conjuring memories of simpler times.

Savoring each bite, Harper found a fleeting solace from the relentless pressures of his current reality. He lingered in the car, reminiscing about a sunny Saturday morning spent with Denise and their children, Alice and James Jr., eagerly exploring rows of minivans at a dealership not unlike this one.

***

Under the midday sun, Harper pulled into the dealership lot, Denise by his side and their children bubbling with excitement in the backseat.

"Dad, look at all the cars!" James Jr. pressed his nose against the window, eyes wide with wonder.

Alice, ever composed, spotted a shiny red minivan near the entrance. "Does that one have the TV screens, Mom?"

Denise smiled at her children's enthusiasm. "Let's find out together."

Exiting the car, they were greeted warmly by Robert, a friendly salesman eager to assist.

"Welcome! How can I help your family today?"

"We're in the market for a spacious family vehicle," Harper replied, his gaze sweeping over the options. "Something loaded with features for the kids."

Robert led them to a row of minivans, highlighting one that met their criteria. Opening the door to a silver van, Alice and James Jr. eagerly climbed inside, marveling at the built-in Blu-ray player and fold-down screen.

"Whoa, look at this, Alice!" James Jr. exclaimed.

"And it has USB ports for our tablets!" Alice added, her eyes sparkling.

Harper and Denise exchanged approving glances as Robert continued his pitch, detailing the van's roomy interior and advanced safety features.

"Why don't you take it for a test drive?" Robert suggested warmly. "I'm sure it'll exceed your expectations."

Denise nodded eagerly. "That sounds perfect. Let's give it a try."

As Harper started the engine and eased away from the dealership, Denise's hand rested gently on his arm. "I think this is the one, Harper. The kids love it, and it has everything we need."

A warm smile spread across Harper's face. "Yeah, I agree. This feels right for our family."

***

Harper's nostalgic reverie was abruptly interrupted by a persistent knock on his car window. Startled, he looked up to find a salesman waiting.

Exiting the vehicle, Harper was greeted warmly. "Good afternoon, sir. Are you looking for something specific today?"

"Yeah," Harper replied, scanning the lot. "I'm thinking about switching to an electric vehicle."

"That's an excellent choice! Here at ElecVe, we have a wide range of models," the salesman enthused, leading Harper towards the latest offerings. "This S model here offers superb performance and advanced features."

Harper rubbed his chin thoughtfully, checking his phone to confirm it matched Carlos Delgado's car model. "Looks good. Can I take it for a test drive?"

"Of course," the salesman nodded, guiding him to a sleek silver vehicle under the dealership's bright lights. The car's glossy exterior gleamed, promising efficiency and style.

"Before we go, I'll need to make a copy of your ID," the salesman explained, leading Harper to a small office nearby. "Just standard procedure."

Handing over his driver's license, Harper watched as it was swiftly scanned and copied. They returned to the car moments later.

"Feel the touchless entry and enjoy the comfort," the salesman invited, opening the driver's side door with a flourish. Harper settled into the plush leather seat, taking in the high-tech dashboard and minimalist interior. The scent of new car leather and freshener created an inviting atmosphere.

"Mind if I connect my phone?" Harper asked, placing his phone in the docking station and starting the pairing process. The car's touchscreen lit up, displaying a range of options.

"Go ahead! It's a standout feature," the salesman replied, unaware of Harper's agenda. "This model offers state-of-the-art connectivity, GPS access, and remote control over climate and seat settings."

Harper nodded, navigating the touchscreen while discreetly accessing the car's onboard system. Real-time data streamed onto his device—location, speed, battery levels—an invaluable resource for his plan.

"Let's take it for a spin," the salesman suggested, pointing to the start button.

Harper pressed it, and the car hummed to life silently. The electric motor purred as Harper eased onto the highway. They accelerated smoothly, merging with traffic effortlessly. Harper glanced at the digital display, monitoring the car's performance metrics and noting its responsive handling.

"Notice how quiet it is?" the salesman remarked. "That's the benefit of electric. Plus, it's eco-friendly and saves on gas."

They exited onto a winding road that overlooked the Industrial District and Rolling Peaks in the distance. The car navigated the curves with its regenerative braking system subtly recharging the battery as they descended.

Returning to the dealership, Harper parked and thanked the salesman, masking his true intentions.

"So, ready to make a purchase?" the salesman asked eagerly.

Harper forced a smile. "It's great. I need to think it over and check a few things first."

"Take your time," the salesman replied, handing Harper a business card. "Feel free to contact me with any questions."

Harper nodded, pocketing the card as he walked away.

Back in his room, Harper decrypted the data from the test drive. The car's proprietary system posed challenges, but with determination, he developed a program to exploit its communication protocols.

Late into the night, Harper refined the program, aiming for remote access. The advanced features that once sold Delgado on the car now presented vulnerabilities. But he needed one more piece—a return to work, or his office, for critical information.

CHAPTER 13: CARLOS DELGADO

The next morning, Harper drove to his office in the TechUse building, returning after a week's absence. Stepping inside, the familiar surroundings provided a brief respite from his life's turmoil. The air carried the rich scent of freshly brewed coffee, mingling with the hum of conversations and the soft clatter of keyboards. His mission was clear: retrieve crucial notes from his desk to finalize an application designed to hack into electric vehicle tracking systems, aiming to trace Delgado's movements.

Navigating through the cybersecurity department's maze of cubicles, Harper finally reached his cluttered yet meticulously organized workspace. Among the papers and office supplies, a photo of his family—Denise, Alice, and James Jr.—smiled back at him, accompanied by personal keepsakes: a drawing of a cat playing with yarn and a small figurine wearing a police uniform. They grounded him, reminding him of his purpose amidst his professional duties.

Rummaging through a desk drawer, Harper's fingers sifted through papers until he found the sought-after notes. As he straightened up, he sensed someone approaching. Turning, Harper met Seraphin's commanding presence. Impeccably dressed and exuding confidence, Seraphin had recently taken charge of the company and always seemed to analyze Harper with a subtle intensity.

"Harper," Seraphin greeted smoothly. "How are you holding up?"

Forcing a small smile, Harper replied, "I'm managing, Mr. Seraphin. Just picking up a few things."

Seraphin's gaze fell on the notes in Harper's hand, curiosity piqued. "What have you got there?"

Harper collected his thoughts. "Just some notes for an app I'm working on. It's meant to track electric vehicles."

Raising an eyebrow in interest, Seraphin took the notes, scanning them with thoughtful consideration before returning them. "This is quite ambitious. What inspired this project?"

Harper shrugged modestly. "Just a personal interest. Thought it could be useful. Helps keep my mind occupied."

A knowing smile touched Seraphin's lips. "Indeed. Sometimes the most useful tools stem from personal necessity. You know, twenty years ago, I was in your shoes, working on cutting-edge tech to carve out my place in this world. If you're looking to enhance efficiency, consider integrating a machine learning algorithm. It could predict vehicle movements based on data trends."

Harper's mind sparked with ideas. "A machine learning algorithm... That's a great suggestion. Thank you, Mr. Seraphin."

With a satisfied smile, Seraphin nodded. "Happy to help. Take care, Harper. I look forward to seeing your progress."

As Seraphin departed, leaving Harper with a sense of unease and newfound inspiration, Harper tucked the notes into his bag and left the office, his thoughts racing ahead to the implementation of Seraphin's suggestion. The encounter replayed in his mind, tinged with a hint of foreboding.

Watching Seraphin stride away, Harper couldn't shake the feeling that their meeting held a deeper purpose. Seraphin's advice on the machine learning algorithm wasn't mere coincidence; it was precisely the catalyst Harper needed to elevate his project. Yet, the question lingered: why had Seraphin shared this insight so readily? The gleam in Seraphin's eyes hinted at an obsession with technology that Harper couldn't fully understand but felt eerily drawn to.

Refocusing, Harper steeled himself against the unease creeping in. Securing the papers in his bag, he left the office, already plotting the algorithm's integration into his application.

***

Harper focused intensely on Delgado's imminent visit to South Valley's warehouses. Parking his car discreetly near the outskirts, he meticulously readied his equipment while monitoring surveillance feeds.

After ensuring his device synchronized with Delgado's anticipated arrival time, Harper approached the main gate with calculated confidence. Engaging the guard, he adopted the guise of a lost traveler seeking directions.

"Excuse me," Harper began casually, "could you help me? My GPS insists on a route through here, but I need to get to the opposite side. Is there an alternative route?"

The guard's response was gruff and dismissive. "Turn around and get lost. This isn't a welcome center."

Harper persisted, maintaining his composure as he stalled, aware of Delgado's silver car approaching from behind. Keeping the guard engaged, Harper positioned himself strategically, ensuring proximity to Delgado to initiate the hack.

Tension spiked suddenly as the guard brandished his SMG, aiming it at Harper.

"Okay, okay, relax," Harper said, his tone placating. "I'll turn around."

Delgado's horn blared behind him as Harper maneuvered his vehicle. Delgado's car passed by, the man casting a suspicious glance at Harper.

Driving a few miles away, Harper parked and monitored his laptop closely. Data streamed steadily, confirming the successful breach. Now armed with real-time access to Delgado's vehicle—its location, speed, internal cameras, and remote driving functions—Harper prepared for the next phase of his plan.

**

Disorder churned in Detective Andrews' mind as he sifted through the latest intelligence on the White Dagger Triad (WDT). His desk was cluttered with detailed reports and photographs, forming a mosaic of suspicion around Jin Tao's organization. Despite its official guise as a legitimate weapons and ammunition manufacturer, Andrews suspected illicit activities beneath the surface. The recent attack on the Cartwrights wasn't their first suspected operation; shell casings engraved with "WDT" recovered from the scene and other incidents over the past month left no doubt about the Triad's involvement. Photographs from these scenes depicted a chilling precision characteristic of seasoned professionals.

Within the intelligence folder lay grainy surveillance images allegedly depicting the leader of the WDT, a shadowy figure believed to be Jin Tao, skilled at eluding direct camera angles. An anonymous tip, accompanied by a tense voice recording, revealed clandestine shipments escorted by armed men during unconventional hours. Andrews felt the weight of these clues tightening like a noose, urging him to connect the dots.

His eyes settled on a large map pinned to the wall, detailing Foundry Hills' labyrinth of streets and alleys infiltrated by the Triad's influence. On the East side, business fronts nestled within Rolling Peaks marked their stronghold. The map delineated narrow lanes weaving through dense residential blocks, punctuated by tattoo parlors, smoke shops, and bars. Andrews possessed an intimate knowledge of these streets, each corner a memory etched from childhood in Foundry Hills—a stark contrast to the bustling skyscrapers of the city center and the neglected outskirts.

Rolling Peaks presented a deceptive tranquility, its panoramic vistas veiling the illicit activities unfolding below. It epitomized the city's dual nature—where natural beauty juxtaposed urban decay, a place where light and darkness uneasily coexisted.

Amidst Andrews' contemplation, his phone abruptly rang—a call from Captain Gerald Reed. The abrasive tone mirrored Andrews' own urgency as he answered, Reed's voice crackling with impatience.

"Andrews, where are the results on the Cartwright case? The Mayor's hounding me. We need closure, fast."

"Captain, we're on the verge," Andrews responded evenly, masking his frustration. He was acutely aware of the Mayor's relentless pressure, particularly during the election season, where swift results were crucial to bolstering public safety credentials. Navigating the politics within the force was familiar territory for Andrews, where short-term fixes often overshadowed long-term solutions.

Reed's tone sharpened. "The Mayor's patience is wearing thin. We can't afford any more delays."

"I understand, Captain," Andrews replied, reflecting on past instances of budget cuts and resource shortages. The Mayor's fixation on public perception frequently clashed with effective policing—a delicate balance Andrews had honed through years of practiced diplomacy.

Andrews left the station with the evidence securely tucked into his inner coat pocket, headed for Rolling Peaks. His journey took him through affluent districts that gradually gave way to the outskirts, where signs of economic decline were evident in abandoned warehouses and unkempt lots.

Approaching Rolling Peaks, Jin Tao's headquarters came into view—a monolithic structure of concrete and steel guarded by seclusion and armed sentries. Unlike the Industrial District below, Rolling Peaks offered commanding views of the city, beneficial in providing early warning during illegal activities. Perpetual mist cloaked the area, lending an aura of secrecy to Jin Tao's domain. The crisp, cold air carried a faint scent of pine, whispering hidden truths through the trees as Andrews prepared to confront the heart of the Triad's operations.

The Triad's influence had been steadily expanding, yet it had not raised concern until recently. Jin Tao's hidden mansion among the peaks showcased his power and wealth. From this vantage point, he oversaw operations, his mind calculating like a chess strategist. Rolling Peaks' tranquility masked the violence and ambition simmering beneath its surface—a place where nature's beauty met human brutality.

Andrews approached the security gate on foot, flashing his badge for entry.

"Detective Andrews," one guard acknowledged, scrutinizing his credentials. "What business do you have here?"

"I need to speak with Jin Tao," Andrews stated firmly, his resolve steeling against the impending confrontation.

"Wait here," instructed the guard, his voice curt as he relayed a message over the radio. Andrews waited in silence, tension tightening his jaw, until the gate groaned open, granting him entry.

"You may enter," the guard directed, gesturing towards the left. "It's the temple with the red roof."

Inside, Andrews found himself face-to-face with a man dressed in a hanbok—a traditional Korean garment. Its vibrant silk shimmered under the lights, accented by a yellow sash around his waist. The man, bald-headed with a dragon tattoo coiled around a dagger, casually sipped from a decorative teacup adorned with Korean lettering. His commanding presence filled the room as Andrews approached.

"Detective Andrews, I presume," the man greeted, his voice smooth and deliberate. "What brings you to my humble establishment?"

"Jin Tao, I am here investigating the murder of Hector Cartwright. We know you did it," Andrews responded, his voice holding a firm edge. His eyes scanned the surroundings for any telltale signs, ready for whatever might unfold next.

Jin Tao's smile was enigmatic. "Power shifts like the wind in this city, Detective. What you see is merely the surface."

"Enough with the cryptic words. The Cartwrights were not innocent," Andrews countered, frustration lacing his tone. "But why did you do it?"

**

Jin Tao's gaze turned icy. "In Foundry Hills, innocence is rare. Corruption runs deep, even among those who seem untainted. The Cartwrights were a nuisance who knew nothing of wielding such power."

Andrews produced a bag containing a casing marked "WDT" and held it up. "Exactly, which is why you killed them, isn't it? These casings were found beside Hector's men at the scene—eight dead cartel members and Hector himself, poisoned before being burned alive."

Jin Tao's smirk was confident. "Those casings are ubiquitous, Detective. Anyone can acquire them. Just because they bear my mark doesn't mean my men used them. And as for the poison, that's a new clue with no evidentiary value against me. Would you like to purchase some WDT ammunition while you're here?" He signaled to an aide, who brought over a case of identical casings, mocking the accusation.

Anger surged within Andrews. "So you deny any involvement?"

"Denial is irrelevant," Jin Tao replied calmly. "In our world, truth is as fluid as honor. Without evidence, your accusations are just wind. The justice system is often blind to truth, swayed by power and influence."

Andrews left the complex empty-handed, driving away with unresolved questions twirling in his thoughts like a storm. His stride back to the car was purposeful, each step resonating with determination. He slammed the car door forcefully and gripped the steering wheel so tightly that his knuckles turned pale.

Jin Tao's cryptic demeanor at the temple gnawed at Andrews. He sensed that the Triad leader was hiding crucial information, yet without tangible evidence, he felt frustrated. But Andrews remained resolute—he vowed to uncover the proof needed to bring Jin Tao to justice.

As Andrews filled half a glass of whiskey, his thoughts were interrupted by an incoming call.

"Andrews," he answered, his voice colored with annoyance and exhaustion.

"Detective, we have a situation," came the urgent voice of the officer on the line. "Multiple bodies found in the Industrial District. Looks like another hit similar to the Cartwright scene."

Andrews felt a surge of adrenaline. "I'll be there in ten minutes," he replied, snatching his coat and keys.

The night enveloped everything in darkness, a dense blanket of clouds concealing the moon and stars, creating an oppressive atmosphere over the Industrial District. Andrews pulled up to the scene, the police cars' blue and red lights flickering on the rain-soaked pavement. He exited his vehicle, feeling the cold air pierce through his coat as he walked toward the group of officers gathered near the crime scene tape.

"Detective," Officer Davis greeted him, lifting the tape for Andrews to duck under. "You need to see this."

Andrews followed Davis through abandoned warehouses, the air heavy with the stench of industrial waste and decay. They halted at a large loading dock, where the bodies of several Nightshade criminals lay in grotesque positions, evidence of a brutal and efficient execution.

"Same as before," Davis said grimly, pointing to the ground near one of the bodies. Andrews crouched down, his flashlight revealing several shell casings scattered among the blood and debris. Each casing bore the distinctive "WDT" engraving.

Andrews picked up one of the casings, turning it over in his gloved hand. "No other evidence?" he asked, already knowing the answer.

Davis shook his head. "Nothing. No fingerprints, no DNA, no witnesses. We checked the cameras of the adjacent buildings but they were deactivated. The only thing we have are these casings."

Andrews straightened up. This was the second massacre linked to the White Dagger Triad, yet they had been careful to leave no other trace of their presence.

"How many victims?" Andrews asked, scanning the scene.

"Six," Davis replied. "All known members of the Nightshade organization.

Are they being exterminated?"

Andrews nodded, his jaw set in determination. "Not sure, but it sure looks like it. Someone is tired of hiding in the shadows, and I fear this is only going to escalate. Bag these casings and get them to forensics. I want a full analysis, even if it seems redundant. Maybe we'll get lucky and find something missed before."

As the forensic team moved in to collect the evidence, Andrews walked the perimeter of the crime scene, his eyes searching for anything out of place. The Industrial District was a warren of shadows and blind corners, a perfect hunting ground for killers like the WDT.

The bodies, the casings, the eerie silence of the Industrial District—it all pointed to the WDT's ruthless efficiency. But why had they left the casings again? Was it a taunt, a deliberate breadcrumb, or a sign of something more sinister?

Andrews knew he needed to delve deeper, to uncover the link that would connect Jin Tao to these killings beyond the casings. The Triad operated with caution, but even the most meticulous criminals made mistakes. He just had to discover theirs. His thoughts turned to the recent downfall of the Cartwright cartel. The control void created by their demise had undoubtedly caused ripples through the criminal underworld. Could the fall of the Cartwrights have directly influenced the rise of another cartel, or was it Jin Tao leveraging this chaos to solidify his grip on the city?

The WDT's methodical approach to their operations suggested a strategic mastermind orchestrating events from behind the scenes, someone adept at navigating power dynamics. Andrews mulled over the possibility that Jin Tao had orchestrated the Cartwright massacre not merely to assert dominance, but as a calculated maneuver to destabilize a rival, seizing their territory and resources in the process.

He recalled the images of the Cartwright crime scene—the brutal precision, the WDT casings. Each detail hinted at a well-planned assault, designed to send a chilling message to their adversaries. But why leave such incriminating evidence behind? Was it intended as a warning, or perhaps a brazen display of arrogance?

Andrews contemplated the Triad's organizational structure. They functioned with precision, akin to a well-oiled machine where every member had a defined role. Their ability to operate covertly despite their growing influence demonstrated their discipline and the intimidation they wielded over allies and adversaries alike.

If the Triad was indeed capitalizing on the downfall of the Cartwrights, it indicated rapid expansion of their operations. The Industrial District, abundant with warehouses and neglected spaces, offered an ideal backdrop for such endeavors. Andrews visualized the district as a chessboard, each move by the Triad carefully calculated to outwit opponents and secure strategic dominance.

As Andrews pieced together these thoughts, a sense of urgency gripped him. The Triad's ascent to power following the Cartwrights' demise signified more than just a struggle for dominance—it marked a potential upheaval in the city's criminal hierarchy. If Jin Tao managed to consolidate this power, it could spell disaster for Foundry Hills.

Andrews knew that uncovering the Triad's plans and stopping their ascent was more critical than ever. He needed to expose the connections, reveal the true extent of their operations, and bring their leaders to justice. The city's future depended on it.

He needed the evidence that would conclusively tie everything together, proving without doubt that Jin Tao and the White Dagger Triad were responsible for these ruthless killings. The stakes had never been higher, and failure was not an option.

***

Harper sat hunched over his laptop, monitoring Carlos Delgado's movements with a sophisticated digital tracking system. The data revealed Delgado's routines—late-night drives along the cliffs of South Valley, always solitary, without his armed entourage. Delgado spent evenings into the early light at his nightclub, where his interest in men was no secret.

Tonight was no different. Delgado's vehicle traced the familiar path through the city's quiet outskirts, heading toward the club after leaving the compound. Harper initiated his hack, the screen displaying real-time data: Delgado's location, speed, and internal video feed.

Here's a revised passage with more detailed descriptions of the car's movements and Harper's control over it:

With a click of the mouse, Harper's voice cut through the dance music, cold and laden with restrained fury. "Delgado," he growled.

Delgado jerked in his seat, casting frantic glances around the vehicle. "What the hell? Who is this?"

"The man who killed Hector Cartwright," Harper's voice dripped with menace. "You and Nightshade took everything from me. Why?"

Delgado pulled over on the hillside road and tried to use his phone, but the screen went black. Frantically, he attempted to restart it, but Harper had disabled it completely, rendering all attempts for help futile.

"Work, damn phone!" Delgado cursed, his frustration mounting. He tried to turn the vehicle around, but to his horror, it resisted his commands. Harper, through deft manipulation of the controls, forced Delgado's car to obey his will. Fear flashed across Delgado's face as he realized he was no longer in control of his vehicle. Harper had overridden the electronic control unit, turning Delgado's own car into a mobile prison hurtling towards an inevitable fate.

Delgado's voice trembled with desperation. "How is this possible? Who are you?" His hands tightened on the steering wheel, trying in vain to maneuver the vehicle, but it remained unresponsive. Pressing down on the gas and brake pedals yielded no effect—they were as useless as the disabled phone.

"Now that you see I have control of your vehicle, tell me why you murdered my family in Warren Court," Harper demanded firmly.

"We were ordered to by Isabella Vargas," Delgado admitted, his voice tinged with fear. "She commanded us to do it—kill the wife and children, but spare the man. It was her directive, or face total loss within the organization." Delgado's voice revealed reluctance.

Harper's response was sharp. "So, instead, you took everything from me?"

"I didn't do anything but incapacitate you. I didn't kill your family. Isabella did. She shot them dead while I was scrambling to pick Hector's unconscious body off the floor."

"You all share equal blame. You should have killed me... Now, you will join Hector in hell. Don't worry, Isabella will be joining you both there very soon." The vehicle accelerated, pushing past 100 miles per hour.

Delgado's car surged forward, the engine roaring as Harper forced it to speed down the winding hillside road. Delgado's hands clamped onto the steering wheel, knuckles white, as he struggled to regain control. The car swerved sharply to the left, tires screeching against the asphalt, throwing Delgado against the door. He grunted in pain, a bruise forming on his shoulder.

"No! Wait!" Delgado pleaded, gripping the steering wheel tightly. The car jerked right, narrowly missing a guardrail as it barreled down the steep incline. Harper's precise commands made the vehicle lurch and veer, every movement deliberate and torturous.

Delgado's heart pounded in his chest as the car sped through a tight curve, the G-forces pressing him into the seat. He tried to brake, but the pedal remained unresponsive. Harper manipulated the controls to simulate a brake failure, sending the car skidding dangerously close to the edge of the road. Delgado screamed as the car fishtailed, the rear tires losing traction on the loose gravel.

The vehicle stabilized momentarily, only for Harper to engage the emergency brake, causing it to screech to a violent halt. Delgado's head snapped forward, slamming into the steering wheel. Blood trickled from a gash on his forehead, mixing with the sweat that drenched his face.

Harper released the brake, and the car shot forward again, accelerating with terrifying speed. Delgado's vision blurred as the vehicle tore through another sharp bend, the centrifugal force pressing him painfully against the door. He gasped for breath, the air thick with the scent of burning rubber.

Desperation clawed at Delgado as the car hurtled toward a narrow bridge spanning a deep ravine. Delgado's attempts to steer were futile, his muscles straining against the unyielding force of the electronic override.

In a final act of defiance, Delgado slammed his fist against the dashboard, but it was no use. The car rocketed onto the bridge, its speed increasing as Harper pushed it to its limits. The structure shuddered under the impact, the steel cables vibrating with the strain.

In an uncontrollable surge of rage and anguish, Harper sent Delgado's vehicle hurtling off the cliff's edge. The car launched into the air, suspended in a moment of horrifying silence before gravity took hold. It plunged into the chasm, the sounds of metal grinding and glass shattering echoing violently as it rolled and descended.

Harper listened, grim and fascinated, to Delgado's desperate screams overpowering the roar of the plummeting vehicle. The video feed flickered with static, but the chaotic sounds were unmistakable. Delgado's cries turned to gagging, his breaths ragged and desperate.

The collision below resembled a symphony of destruction—metal screeching, glass shattering, and the explosion's deafening roar transforming into a burning abyss at the ravine's bottom. Delgado's final, agonized breath gurgled in Harper's ears, a faint echo of retribution achieved.

Harper watched the flickering screen displaying the smoldering wreckage. It was done. He turned the screens off, but a sudden knocking at the door startled him. Opening it cautiously, he found nothing but a quiet hallway. As he started to close the door, a sharp, stabbing pain lanced through his skull, radiating from his temples to the back of his head. He winced, pressing a hand to his forehead as his vision blurred and dark spots expanded before his eyes. The pain was excruciating, far worse than before.

Breaths came in shallow, ragged gasps, each one a struggle against the mounting pressure in his head. He could feel his pulse pounding in his temples, the rhythm erratic and relentless. The room seemed to spin around him, the light growing dimmer, and he swayed unsteadily in his chair.

Harper's hand trembled as he reached out, closing the lid of the laptop with a soft click. He squeezed his eyes shut, attempting to will the pain away, but it only intensified, pushing him towards unconsciousness.

Sweat beaded on his forehead, and a wave of nausea rose in his throat. His thoughts became disjointed, fragmented by the relentless agony overwhelming him. He didn't understand what was happening, but the fear of losing control, of being unable to continue his mission, ate away at his consciousness.

Clutching his head, Harper staggered to his feet, his vision narrowing to a pinprick of light. He stumbled towards the bathroom, the pain blurring his senses and dulling his awareness of his surroundings. Collapsing onto the cold tile floor, he curled into a fetal position, his body convulsing as the pain reached its peak. The room spun around him, and he felt himself slipping away, his vision fading into darkness.

Chapter 14: Anguish: Past And Present

In his remote workspace, the soft glow of a desk lamp illuminated the grim photographs spread before Andrews. Each image depicted unbridled violence—a massacre marked by bodies strewn across the ground, perforated with bullet holes, capturing the ruthlessness of the assailants.

Andrews rose from his desk and walked to the kitchen, his movements deliberate, his mind haunted by the faces in the photos and the unfinished business that gnawed at him. He poured himself a generous glass of whiskey, the amber liquid clinking against the ice cubes. The first sip burned as it slid down his throat, momentarily easing the sharp edges of his thoughts but failing to silence the memories that persisted. He removed a black name tag with silver lettering from his pocket, rolling it between his fingers. The name "S. Andrews" glinted in the light.

***

Alone at home, engrossed in a video game, Shawn Jr. had been eagerly awaiting his father's return from his patrol shift. The sudden ring of the doorbell shattered the ambiance, pulling him from the virtual world. Peeking through the plastic curtains, he spotted Mark and Wayne, fellow officers from his father's precinct, their strained smiles and uneasy glances signaling impending bad news.

"Hey, Shawn, may we come in?" Mark's voice carried a somber undertone. They led him to the living area, where Shawn Jr. sensed the tense atmosphere. Finally, Mark spoke, his voice trembling with sorrow. "Shawn, your dad was in an incident... an officer-involved shooting," he faltered, the weight of the words settling heavily. "He didn't make it. He was trying to stop a robbery and got shot. He died on the way to Foundry Hospital."

Shock numbed Shawn Jr.'s senses, muting the attempts at comfort. He didn't register the dropped controller or the voices of Mark and Wayne. All he could hear was the pounding of his own heart, a relentless drumbeat marking the loss of his father. In the days that followed, he struggled, grappling with the void left by his father's sudden absence. His grades plummeted, his once-bright demeanor dulled by grief and confusion. Alone in the school playgrounds, he sought solace in isolation, haunted by memories of happier times with his dad.

Raised in foster care, stability had been a luxury Shawn Jr. rarely knew. His early years were marked by placements with neglectful foster families, some exploiting the system for profit, others well-meaning but unable to tame his growing rebellious streak. By age 17, he found himself caught in a cycle of minor offenses, a path seemingly leading nowhere.

It was during one of these troubled moments that Shawn Jr. encountered Officer Mark. Recognizing the boy as Shawn Sr.'s son, Mark saw beyond the troubled facade to a young man in need of guidance. In a heart-to-heart conversation, Mark shared stories of Shawn Sr.'s dedication and integrity, offering Shawn Jr. a glimpse into the father he had lost and the man he could become.

Mark took Shawn Jr. under his wing, mentoring him through the challenges with patience and understanding. He passed on Shawn Sr.'s name tag, a symbol of trust and a reminder of the legacy he carried. As Shawn Jr. began to see a path forward, Mark's influence grew, shaping him into a determined young man with a renewed sense of purpose.

Now known as Detective Andrews, Shawn Jr. had risen through the ranks with a determination born from adversity. His journey from grief-stricken youth to respected officer was a testament to resilience and the guiding hand of a mentor who saw beyond his troubled past.

**

Andrews slowly opened his eyes, disoriented and lying on the floor amidst the remnants of his evening—a discarded whiskey bottle and scattered reports. His pocket vibrated, and he pulled out his phone, noting the missed calls and a waiting voicemail.

Ignoring it for now, he stumbled to the bathroom, his head pounding despite his usual tolerance for alcohol. The cold water hit him like a slap, but he welcomed the shock, hoping it would wash away the toxins. Standing under the stream, he closed his eyes, letting the water cascade over him until he felt somewhat sober.

Exiting the shower, he dried off and wrapped a towel around his waist. As he brushed his teeth, he glanced at the clock—it was just past 11 a.m. He retrieved his typical outfit from the wardrobe: a white button-down shirt, black trousers, and a tie. After dressing, he attached his badge to his belt, secured his shoulder holster, and placed his gun in it from beside the bed.

His thoughts returned to Jin Tao and the WDT, convinced that they were behind the recent killings. Andrews played the voicemail. "Andrews! This is Capt. Reed. We need you here ASAP. Call me when you get this."

Curiosity mingled with duty as Andrews pondered the unexpected summons. He slipped on his leather coat, grabbed his keys, and hurried out the door. During the drive, he returned Captain Reed's call. "Captain, what's going on?"

"Andrews, we've got a situation," Reed's voice crackled through the speaker, brimming with urgency. "Carlos Delgado's car was found at the bottom of Rolling Peaks. It's bad."

"What do you mean, bad?" Andrews asked, his curiosity rising.

Reed's tone turned grim. "Bad as in he's dead. Looks like he lost control of the vehicle and it veered off the cliff. I need you down here, now! I'm on my way back to the station, but Griggs and Martinez are already on the scene. They can brief you."

"Got it, I should be there in about 20 minutes." Andrews said before ending the call. He got on the expressway, heading towards Rolling Peaks. The commute felt short as he focused intently on the case.

***

Andrews arrived at a scene of controlled chaos. Emergency vehicles crowded the area, their lights casting eerie flashes against the rugged cliffs. Smoke still wisped from the mangled wreckage below, a grim demonstration to the violence of Delgado's fatal crash. Without hesitation, Andrews descended the treacherous path on foot, making his way to the scattered remains of the car.

Sergeant Griggs, one of the initial responders, approached him. "Detective, it's a mess down here. Looks like he lost control on the turn above."

Andrews paused, thoughtfully surveying the wreckage. "Is there any indication of what caused him to lose control? Maybe a distraction?"

Officer Martinez joined them, having overheard the conversation. "Preliminary assessment suggests it was a solo accident. There have been no signs of foul play so far."

Andrews frowned, crouching near the twisted metal. "Delgado was cautious. This doesn't add up. It's too convenient."

Martinez scratched his head, his expression troubled. "I get what you're saying, but without concrete evidence…"

Before he could finish, their attention was diverted to the medics transporting a stretcher across the rocky terrain. The rough landscape caused an arm to slip out momentarily, revealing an Eclipse tattoo—the symbol of the Nightshade syndicate.

Andrews' focus was interrupted by the vibrations of his phone. It was an incoming call from Berg.

"Hey Berg, I'm busy right now at a crime scene in Rolling Peaks," he said.

"Actually, it's about that," she exclaimed. "Late last night, the car sent out an SOS. Usually, this happens after a crash, but this… this occurred before the crash."

"Okay, so a malfunction maybe?" Andrews asked.

"No," Berg replied. "After digging further, we found that there was an override just before the SOS was sent out. The override took over the vehicle's ECU."

"ECU?"

"Sorry, it's the Electronic Control Unit. Basically, Carlos didn't have control of anything. The car was driven remotely."

"Damn it." Andrews muttered, glancing back at the wreckage. He turned sharply to Martinez, his eyes hard and focused. "Get a team down there. Sweep the area for any devices that might have hijacked Delgado's car. This wasn't an accident."

"Andrews, this was all done remotely," Berg interjected, her tone laced with fascination. "The killer used the vehicle's technology. There won't be anything there to find."

"Thanks, Berg. Let me know if there is anything else," Andrews said.

"You're welcome," Berg replied before disconnecting the call.

Andrews climbed back up the rocky path to the road, his mind churning with possibilities. Who possessed the technical prowess to orchestrate such a move? Jin Tao and the WDT crossed his mind. However, this method seemed out of their usual playbook and above their level of expertise.

His phone rang again, this time it was Capt. Reed. "What's the status on Delgado's accident?"

"Captain, this wasn't an accident. Delgado's car was remotely driven off the cliff."

"What? How?" Reed's tone was grave.

"Berg and her team have the full details. And sir, this may be connected to Hector's murders as well. The link is the hacking of technology."

"What do you mean? Wasn't Hector and his crew massacred?"

"Well, yes, but there were also hacks involved. There has to be a third player."

"Okay, just keep me updated. The mayor's going to be breathing down my neck on this."

"I will, Captain," Andrews affirmed, ending the call.

He stared out over the cliffs, perplexed by it all. On the drive back to the station, he thought about the deaths of Delgado and Cartwright. Both cases shared a chilling similarity—executed by someone with technical expertise.

Back at the station, Andrews sifted through yet another report of violence attributed to the WDT. "Another armed robbery, this time in the

Industrial District," he quietly remarked, pinpointing the location on a map already dotted with red pins. "They're getting bolder."

A knock on the door pulled his attention. Detective Ramirez entered holding a stack of fresh reports.

"This is getting out of hand," Ramirez said, placing the papers on the already cluttered desk. "WDT hit three more drug distribution points last night. They're moving fast."

Andrews rubbed his temples; the cases were mounting and they were not making any headway. "Any leads? Witnesses?"

Ramirez shook his head. "Nothing for certain. Several witnesses were identified but they are too scared to talk. We've tried to reason with them, offering witness protection, but the WDT's influence is too strong. It wouldn't surprise me if they were getting paid to keep quiet."

Andrews let out a frustrated sigh. "We need something, Ramirez. Anything we can use to bring these bastards down."

"We're doing everything we can," Ramirez replied, though his tone carried the same frustration. "But they cover their tracks well. It is possible to bring them in one by one and shake them up, but without evidence, their attorney Sanchez will eat us up in court."

Andrews nodded, realizing their battle against the WDT was only just beginning. "You're right. What if we bring Sanchez in and make some sort of arrangement? He's been loyal to Nightshade; maybe he'll help us keep WDT at bay."

Ramirez agreed. "Not a bad idea, Andrews. I'll try to arrange a discreet meeting with him."

"Sounds like a plan. For now, let's check with Capt. Reed about increasing patrols at Rolling Peaks. We'll find a crack in their armor sooner or later."

***

Harper's eyes fluttered open, and he groaned, trying to make sense of his surroundings. The features of his hotel room gradually sharpened into view, but something felt off. He struggled to sit up, his body heavy and uncooperative.

As his eyes adjusted to the darkness, he perceived a silhouette by his bed.

"Denise?" he asked, his voice weak.

"No, Harper, it's me, Margaret," the woman said softly, anxiety evident on her face. The familiar voice of his neighbor brought him back to reality.

Confusion clouded his mind. "What happened?" he croaked, his throat dry and scratchy.

Margaret leaned closer, her expression gentle yet worried. "The door to your room was open, and I got worried. I found you unconscious on the bathroom floor. I called for help from a hotel employee, and we brought you to the bed. You've been out for a while."

Harper tried to recollect the sequence of events that preceded his loss of consciousness, but his memory was a blurred and disordered mess. He had a faint recollection of the bathroom and the throbbing headaches, but beyond that, his memory was blank.

Margaret's voice broke through his thoughts. "You were muttering in your unconsciousness, Harper. You said, 'No, Denise. Alice and James Jr., don't leave me.'" Her eyes softened with sympathy.

The mention of his wife and children's names cut into his heart like a sharp blade. He shut his eyes, inhaling deeply, readying himself to release the burden from his soul.

Harper began. "Denise, Alice, and James Jr. They were everything to me, and they were taken from me in the most brutal way."

Margaret reached out, placing a comforting hand on his arm. "What happened, Harper?"

Harper swallowed hard, the memories flooding back with painful clarity. "It was a home invasion. They forced their way in... They didn't come to talk. They just wanted to take them away from me."

Margaret's eyes filled with tears. "Oh, Harper, I'm so sorry."

Harper nodded, his grief momentarily lifting as he shared his burden. Margaret squeezed his arm gently. "You don't have to go through this alone, Harper. Your friends, your neighbors, we can help you."

"Thank you, Margaret. Your support means a lot to me," he said, his voice steadier now. "But I need to go somewhere. There's something I have to do."

"Harper, are you sure you're ready to go out? You just regained consciousness." She replied, expressing her concern.

He nodded. "I appreciate your concern, but this is something I have to do."

"Alright, Harper. Just promise me you'll be careful."

Harper gave her a small, grateful smile. "I will. Thank you, Margaret, for looking out for me."

As he stepped out, Margaret watched him go, hoping he would find the strength he needed to face whatever lay ahead.

***

Harper knelt before the graves of his wife, daughter, and son at the Foundry Hills Cemetery. The headstones stood solemnly against the dull sky, and he gently placed red peonies in front of them. His fingers lingered on the cold stone as he whispered softly, "I miss you all so much. This road I'm on… it will all be over soon."

A routine calm drifted over the cemetery, broken only by the rustle of leaves and distant birdsong. The deaths of Hector Cartwright and Carlos Delgado weighed heavy on Harper's mind—not with guilt, but with a thirst for justice. Vengeance was the bitter solace that filled the void in his heart, or so he believed.

"I thought this would make it better," he whispered. "But I feel more lost than ever. This town… no place will ever be home."

He closed his eyes, letting seconds pass as he wondered what the end had in store for him. When he opened them, he saw his children standing there, their faces solemn.

"Dad, why are you doing this?" James Jr. asked in an innocent voice.

"Because they took you from me," Harper replied, his voice breaking. "They took all of you. I have to make them pay."

Alice shook her head, her eyes filled with sadness. "We want you to be happy, not hurt. Remember what you told me when I cried after falling off my bike? You said a scar may be expected, but it shouldn't keep you from getting back on. So, mourn for us, it's expected, but you have to move on."

Harper felt a lump in his throat as the vision of his children faded. "I'll try," he whispered.

As Harper rose, a sharp pain pierced his head, an unwelcome visitor in his already burdened mind. He winced, pressing a hand to his temple. Struggling against the pain, he wandered through the cemetery, his gaze drifting until he spotted Andrews standing by another grave. The detective's stoic presence resonated with Harper, a reminder that even relentless pursuers had their own ghosts haunting them.

They had met before at the hospital, and Harper briefly wondered about Andrews' loss, the anguish etched into his every movement.

Compassion was no longer a part of Harper's world. He left the cemetery, unbound in his relentless quest for retribution.

Harper wandered the streets of Foundry Hills, and the city felt different—darker and more dangerous with the rise of the WDT. He couldn't shake the feeling that the violence he had unleashed was spiraling out of control.

Turning a corner, he spotted a man loitering near a closed storefront. The man was tall, with a muscular build and a menacing presence. Harper's instincts kicked in, and he studied the stranger more closely. There was something familiar about him, but Harper couldn't quite figure it out until he got closer.

As Harper walked past, he noticed a tattoo peeking out from under the man's sleeve—a dagger entwined with a snake. Harper's heart skipped a beat. He had seen that symbol before in reports about the White Dagger Triad. But this man wasn't dressed in the typical garb; he was blending in, hiding in plain sight.

Harper's conscience was overwhelmed with remorse and exasperation. He couldn't shake off the belief that the rise of the WDT was a consequence of his own actions. The Nightshade organization had been merciless, yet they paled in comparison to the monstrous nature of the WDT. It dawned on him that his efforts to dismantle one evil had unintentionally bolstered another. The man caught Harper's stare and gave a slight nod before walking away, disappearing into the crowd.

***

Andrews stood beside his father's grave, the environment around him foggy and distorted. The cold air bit at his skin, but he hardly felt it, his perception numbed by the whiskey coursing through his bloodstream.

He swayed slightly on his feet, his gaze fixed on the gravestone before him. Carved into the granite was the name "Shawn Andrews Sr.," a permanent tribute to the man who had shaped his life, even in death. The pain of his absence was a constant companion, a wound that never fully healed.

With a heavy sigh, Andrews sank to his knees, the bottle of whiskey slipping from his grasp and thudding softly against the ground. He stared at the tombstone, his anger and sadness boiling over.

"I was fourteen," he slurred, his voice thick with emotion. "Why did you leave me? Why did you have to be the hero? And look, look where it got you!" He paused, taking another swig from the bottle. "I was just a boy, left to pick up the pieces. Now look at me. The only family I have is in this bottle, numbing the pain I've kept inside for so long."

He wiped at his eyes with the back of his hand, the motion clumsy and uncoordinated. The world seemed to spin around him, but he forced himself to focus on the gravestone, on the memory of his father.

"But I'm trying to live up to your legacy, Dad. I'm trying to make sure no one else has to go through what I did."

He took a deep, shuddering breath. "I won't let them down," he vowed, his voice barely more than a whisper. "I won't let them suffer like I did. I'll protect them and make you proud."

The sorrow caused by his father's passing, combined with the burden of guilt and remorse that had lingered within him for many years, was a heavy load to bear. But even in his drunken state, Andrews knew he couldn't give up.

He pushed himself to his feet, the world spinning around him, swaying unsteadily. "I'll make you proud, I promise," he whispered. With one last glance at the grave, Andrews turned and walked towards the town, determined to carry on.

Chapter 15: Unlikely Alliances

Casting a quick glance at his wrist, Harper noted the sun sinking lower in the sky and the city's vibrant nightlife beginning to awaken. His hotel room was just a short distance away. Lost in his thoughts, he strode with purpose until a sudden movement captured his attention—a child innocently stepping onto the road while her parent, distracted by a phone, remained oblivious to the oncoming car.

His eyes widened as he took in the situation. Without hesitation, he broke into a sprint, legs pumping furiously as he closed the distance. Each step felt like a lifetime, the sound of the approaching car growing louder in his ears.

In a desperate lunge, he reached out and grabbed the child, yanking her back with all his strength. The car zoomed by a split second later, its side mirror colliding violently with his shoulder. The impact sent a sharp pain through his arm and caused his breath to catch.

Wincing, he felt his shoulder throbbing from the collision. Quickly turning towards the woman, he saw her face contorted in shock as she took in the scene, her phone slipping from her fingers and clattering to the ground.

"Watch your kid!" Harper's voice was raw with adrenaline, his eyes flashing with the intensity of the moment. "What the hell is wrong with you? You're too busy on your phone to see your daughter almost get hit by a car!"

The woman's eyes filled with tears as she clutched her child tightly, her grip trembling. Tears streamed down her face, her expression a mix of terror and relief. Her phone lay forgotten on the ground, a symbol of her negligence.

"Next time, she might not be so lucky. Don't let her suffer because of your negligence." Harper surveyed the scene, feeling a resurgence of pain in his head as his eyes scanned the street. In a brief instant, he believed he caught sight of his wife, daughter, and son standing outside a familiar café they used to frequent, their expressions filled with tranquility. However, as he blinked, they vanished, leaving him disoriented amidst the moving crowd.

Surrounded by onlookers, their voices a mixture of admiration and worry, Harper found himself at the center of attention.

"You saved her!"

"That was incredible!"

He nodded, his thoughts still in disarray, accepting their appreciation with modest gratitude. A police officer appeared, his face serious as he evaluated the scene.

"Are you alright, sir? That was quite an impact," the officer commented, glancing at the broken mirror on the pavement before returning his look to Harper.

"I'll be alright," Harper assured, his voice strained as he adjusted his jacket to conceal the discomfort. "There's no need for a statement; it was just an accident. I simply want to get home and ice my shoulder."

The officer paused, worry evident on his face, holding the radio as though he was on the verge of relaying the incident. "Are you certain?"

Shaking his head faintly, Harper replied, "I'm fine, really. Just need some rest."

"Alright," the officer conceded reluctantly. "If you change your mind, here's my card. I can take the statement later."

Harper took the card. "Thanks, officer, I appreciate it." Slipping the card into his pocket, his eyes briefly met the officer's. "I'll let you know if I change my mind."

With a final nod, Harper turned and walked away, each step emanating intense agony that surged through his shoulder.

Approaching the hotel, Harper caught sight of his neighbor Margaret stepping out from the entrance. Her eyes widened in surprise as she noticed him, observing that he was cradling his shoulder.

"Harper, what's wrong?" she asked, her worry apparent.

"Just a minor mishap, Margaret," Harper responded with a forced grin, silently grateful for her concern.

"Let me help. That shoulder doesn't look good," Margaret insisted, her worry deepening.

Harper shook his head, giving a dismissive wave. "I'll be fine, really. Thanks for your concern."

Margaret frowned but didn't press further. "Very well, but remember, if you need anything, do not hesitate to contact me."

"I will, thank you, Margaret." Harper replied, offering a smile before retreating into his hotel room.

Once inside, he carefully removed his jacket and shirt, revealing a shoulder that was both bruised and swollen. Harper grabbed a towel, soaked it in cold water, and pressed it against his shoulder, finding some relief in the cold sensation. As he eased himself into a chair, his attention was drawn to the voices coming from the computer. Detective Andrews' audio played through the speakers.

"...Yes, Berg?" Harper tried to catch up to the rest of the audio.

"Andrews, the code used in the warehouse hack matches the patterns from the Delgado incident."

Harper leaned closer, his attention fully captured by the unfolding investigation. His brain buzzed with implications and connections as he listened intently to Berg's findings.

***

Andrews looked up from the computer screen, his brow creasing as he absorbed Berg's report. "Go on," he encouraged, leaning in slightly, his fingers tapping in a rhythmic pattern on the desk.

"It's a sophisticated system, almost like a digital fingerprint," Berg explained, her voice carrying a sense of urgency. Her eyes were wide with the gravity of the situation. "Whoever did this has serious skills. They hijacked the vehicle's auto-drive, disabled GPS tracking, and manipulated the audio—all interconnected. They were operating the car from a remote location with a precision I've never seen."

Andrews leaned back in his chair. "So, we're considering the possibility of a single culprit responsible for both incidents?" he inquired, a mix of curiosity and concern.

"Exactly," Berg affirmed. "And whoever it is, they're highly skilled. This isn't amateur work. They left a trail, but it's subtle, almost like they wanted us to find it, but only if we were clever enough."

Berg pulled up another screen with lines of code and digital footprints highlighted in red. "Look at this," she said, pointing to a cluster of data points. "These patterns are too intricate to be coincidental. They've used a series of proxy servers and encrypted channels, but there are slight variations in the encryption algorithms that match the ones we found in the warehouse hack."

Berg's eyes flicked to Andrews, a hint of fear in her voice. "If they can hack into the warehouse that killed Cartwright or the car that sent Delgado off a cliff, who knows what else they're capable of? We're dealing with a highly dangerous individual, Detective."

Andrews leaned back, folding his arms across his chest. "We need to get ahead of this person. Find out who they are and what their next move is. Double-check every piece of evidence we've collected. Look for any patterns or anomalies we might have missed."

Berg nodded, determination hardening her features. "I'll get the team on it right away. We'll need to run deep background checks on anyone who could possibly have the skills to pull this off."

Just then, Martinez and Sanchez walked into the office, making their way towards Andrews.

"Keep up the great work, Berg. I need to talk to these two," Andrews said.

Berg nodded and headed back to the analyst floor.

"Defense Attorney Sanchez, thanks for seeing us," Andrews greeted.

"This better be good, Andrews," Sanchez replied in a frustrated tone.

"Sanchez, I promise it will be. Martinez, take him to the room so we can chat while I grab some documents."

"You got it, Andrews," Martinez replied, guiding Sanchez to the interview room.

Andrews and Martinez entered the small interview room where Sanchez was already seated, looking slightly impatient. Andrews placed a thick file on the table.

"I apologize for the delay, Sanchez," Andrews began, sitting across from him. "We appreciate you coming in."

Sanchez folded his arms, his eyes narrowing. "Let's get this over with. What do you need?"

Martinez leaned against the wall, arms crossed, watching the interaction closely.

"Straight to the point, good," Andrews replied. He opened the file and laid out several photos on the table. The first showed Cartwright, lifeless in his warehouse, burned to a crisp. The second displayed Delgado, also burned, slumped in his car. Sanchez's eyes flickered with recognition and something akin to fear, but his leg kept jiggling.

"You recognize these men, don't you?" Andrews asked, his voice calm but probing. "Cartwright and Delgado. Both dead. Both tied to the Nightshade organization."

Sanchez's jaw tightened, but he remained silent.

"And you know as well as we do," Andrews continued, "that it's only a matter of time before Isabella is next on the list. The WDT is cleaning house, and you're deep in Nightshade. Your pockets are thinning out with each of these deaths."

Martinez stepped forward, his tone more urgent. "Look, we know you hate the WDT as much as we do. They're a common enemy. Help us take them down, and you might just save what's left of the organization and Isabella."

Sanchez shifted his gaze back and forth between the two detectives, contemplating their request. "And what exactly do you need me to do?"

Andrews leaned in, his gaze intense. "We need you to wear a wire and get close to Jin Tao. Get him to incriminate himself and his organization. Tie him to the recent crimes and the murder of Cartwright. You're in a position to do this, and it's your best shot at keeping Nightshade alive. We believe they are the ones behind the killings."

Sanchez hesitated, his face a mask of conflicting emotions. Eventually, he exhaled sharply, momentarily halting his leg's movement before it resumed. "Alright. I'll do it. But if this goes south…"

"We'll protect you," Andrews interrupted, his tone firm. "We're in this together."

Martinez nodded in agreement. "You get us what we need on Jin Tao, and we'll do what we can to ensure the safety of Isabella."

Sanchez looked at the photos one last time, a resolve settling in his eyes. "Alright. Let's do this."

***

As the sun dipped below the horizon over the docks near Foundry Hills, Isabella Vargas stood at the water's edge, her gaze fixed on the city lights across the bay. The soft lapping of waves against the pier created a rhythmic backdrop. The crisp, salty air carried a chill that did nothing to temper the fire of determination blazing in her eyes.

With her phone pressed to her ear, she spoke tersely. "Go ahead."

"Both Cartwright and Delgado are dead," the voice from the other end expressed with disappointment.

Isabella closed her eyes briefly, drawing in a deep breath to compose herself. The news had already been delivered to her by her associates. Cartwright and Delgado had been pivotal in her network, and their losses raised significant concerns within the organization. "I'll ensure we maintain control," she said, her voice cold and resolute. "I'll take care of the fallout."

***

Isabella ended the call, pocketing her phone as she turned away from the water. Her thoughts drifted to her childhood, to the lessons learned from a father who had ruled his empire with an iron fist. He had taught her that power was everything, and trust was a luxury she could not afford. Rising through the ranks of the Nightshade organization with ruthless competence, she had earned her position not just through loyalty, but through calculated brutality.

Her mind raced with possibilities, assessing allies and identifying threats. She knew she couldn't show any sign of weakness. In the cutthroat world she inhabited, vulnerability was a death sentence. Swift and decisive actions were necessary to fill the void left by Cartwright and Delgado's orchestrated deaths, to solidify her control and eliminate any threats to her power.

A seagull cried overhead, its call piercing the silence of the twilight. Glancing up, she watched the bird's solitary flight against the darkening sky. A kinship with the creature stirred within her, both of them solitary figures navigating a dangerous world. But unlike the seagull, Isabella was not content to simply survive. She was determined to thrive, to conquer.

Pulling her coat tighter against the growing chill, she began walking back to her car, her heels clicking sharply against the wooden planks of the dock. She needed to meet with her most trusted lieutenants to strategize and ensure their loyalty. There could be no room for doubt or hesitation.

She knew exactly who was behind the deaths of Cartwright and Delgado—Harper. He was highly skilled and dangerous, just as Mr. S had warned her. She needed to be even more cunning and ruthless to bring him down and rejoin him with his family. The game of revenge and survival was one she knew well, and she was prepared to play it to the end.

Reaching her black sedan parked under the cover of shadows, Isabella slid into the driver's seat. She started the engine and drove away from the docks, heading northwest towards Rolling Peaks. The sound of an outgoing call played from the car's speakers.

"Isabella, to what do I owe the pleasure?" the voice said.

"Jin, everything is in place, just as he promised us," she replied.

"Good... Let's meet and deal with our outsider. His part in our scheme is approaching its end."

***

Harper groaned as he tried to sit up, wincing at the sharp pain shooting through his shoulder. Rotating it slowly, he felt the tightness and strain with every movement. The morning served as a reminder of yesterday's incident, each motion a struggle. Pushing through his morning routine, he winced as he tried to pour coffee. The mug slipped from his grasp, shattering on the floor. He cursed under his breath, frustration piling on top of his pain.

A knock on the door interrupted his self-pity.

"Harper, are you there?" said a familiar female voice.

Using his good arm, Harper opened the door. Margaret stood there, her brow furrowed with concern.

"Hey, Harper. Just wanted to check in on you. How are you holding up?" she asked, her eyes searching his face.

He gave a faint nod, wincing slightly as his shoulder throbbed. "I'm alright, Margaret. Just a bit sore, but nothing I can't handle."

Her eyes flicked to his shoulder, seeing the strain he tried to hide. "Do you need anything? You look like you are in pain."

She wasn't wrong. "No, I'm good at the moment. It's just a bit of pain, nothing I can't handle."

"Well..." She retrieved something from her bag and revealed a bottle of painkillers. Handing them to him with a gentle smile, she said, "I hurt my shoulder a few years ago playing tennis, and this type of medication was a godsend. Oh, and these are not the ones I got then, I promise," she added with a giggle, attempting to jest.

"Thanks," Harper said, genuinely grateful for her kindness, looking at the pill bottle's label.

"Well, I'm off then. Please don't hesitate to swing by if you need anything, Harper. I mean it."

"Much appreciated. I'll pay you back for these."

She nodded and smiled as she walked away.

Harper closed the door, catching a glimpse of himself in the mirror on the coat closet. The reflection wasn't what he remembered. It was of a damaged and lost man. He carefully tended to his shoulder, grateful for the brief interaction but determined not to let it distract him from his current task.

The mug's debris lay scattered across the kitchen floor, almost mocking him—a reminder that everything he touched or loved seemed to break. Leaving it there for now, he turned instead toward the glow of multiple screens casting a cold light across the room. The sight reminded him of his workplace, a place he hadn't returned to since the incident. It felt like forever since he'd been back to the cubicle, where he could shield others from attacks—something he had been unable to do for his family.

For the past ten years, Harper had worked for the Department of Defense, countering cyber threats. He operated as both blue and red forces in simulated and real-world scenarios, delicately balancing between defending against attacks and launching them. In the battlefield of cyber warfare, where every line of code could mean the difference between success and catastrophe, staying updated with the latest knowledge and maintaining proficiency in coding were crucial.

One of his colleagues, Sam, often marveled at Harper's ability to navigate the crucible of digital warfare. "You're like a ghost in the machine, Harper, or a machine yourself," Sam once said, watching him effortlessly breach a simulated enemy network while simultaneously launching defensive barriers.

Harper joked, "Just doing what needs to be done. Someone needs to keep your social media safe," as he prepared for the next wave of challenges.

Now, though, Harper's focus had shifted. This wasn't about defense anymore; it was about offense. It was about revenge on Nightshade, and specifically, Isabella Vargas.

His phone vibrated, the voicemail notification appearing again. Dialing and listening, he heard, "Harper, this is Dr. Evans from Foundry Hills Medical Center. I'm calling to discuss some findings from your recent lab results that require further investigation. I'd like you to come in for additional tests as soon as possible. It's important that we address this promptly, as it may have significant implications for your health. Please call my office so that we can get you in. Take care."

Strange, he wondered, "Probably just another routine follow-up," he told himself. Aside from the occasional headaches and fatigue, he attributed his symptoms to the stress and exhaustion he had endured since the tragedy. Besides, he didn't have the time right now; perhaps later he would return the call.

His desktop hummed with activity, several programs running in the background. A notification pinged, triggered by his code detecting specific traffic patterns. A clue emerged: a series of messages from Nightshade members pointing to a meeting planned that evening at Linear Stars, a popular upscale nightclub. A meeting the infamous Vargas was scheduled to attend. It was an opportunity he couldn't pass up.

☐

Chapter 16: The Setup

Andrews and Martinez parked their surveillance van in a shadowy corner near the Industrial District, the dim streetlights providing minimal visibility. They kept a vigilant eye out for Sanchez.

A few minutes later, Sanchez walked up, his demeanor casual but his eyes observant. "I parked my car a block away," he said quietly, glancing around. "That's usual protocol, right? I preferred not to draw any suspicion."

Andrews nodded and handed him a small, discreet wire. "We'll tuck this out of sight. You remember the objective? Get Jin Tao to incriminate himself about Hector Cartwright."

He paused, ensuring the wire was well-hidden before continuing. "If anything goes wrong, use the code word 'Stallion' to abort. We'll be listening the whole time. Just stay calm and stick to the plan."

Sanchez nodded, his expression serious. "Got it. Stallion. And get Jin Tao to talk."

Martinez stepped in, his eyes scanning the area. "Alright, everything looks clear out there. Sanchez, we'll be parked nearby. Keep the conversation natural, and don't push too hard. If you feel any danger, use the code word immediately. You sure about this Sanchez?"

Sanchez forced a smile. "Yes, I'll be careful."

Andrews gave him a reassuring pat on the shoulder. "You'll do fine. We've got your back."

With a final nod, Sanchez walked off towards the old factories. He was supposed to meet Jin Tao, but as he stepped in, he was greeted by one of Jin Tao's lieutenants. The man's imposing figure, 6 foot 4, bald head, and cold eyes sent a chill down Sanchez's spine. His neck bore a tattoo, a dragon wrapped around a white dagger.

"Mr. Sanchez," the lieutenant greeted him, motioning towards a dusty table and chairs. "Please, have a seat."

Sanchez sat down, his leg jiggling under the table. "I was expecting Mr. Tao," he said, trying to keep his voice steady.

The lieutenant offered a tight-lipped smile. "Mr. Tao sends his apologies. He's occupied with other matters."

Sanchez nodded, attempting to mask his anxiety. "No problem. So, what can I do to maximize your business? Are you still encountering issues with the police or Nightshade?"

The lieutenant's smile faded. "No, and as a matter of fact, Mr. Tao wishes to express that he is no longer interested in your services."

A different WDT member entered and quietly spoke into the lieutenant's ear. The atmosphere became filled with an uneasy silence.

"Mr. Sanchez, it's time to bid farewell," he stated, gesturing towards the exit.

Sanchez's leg stopped jiggling; it was clear the meeting was over. He rose from his seat, attempting to maintain a nonchalant demeanor. "Well, if you change your mind, you know how to reach me."

The lieutenant nodded but said nothing more. Sanchez made his way back to the van, his heart pounding. He slipped inside the van discreetly and relayed the conversation to Andrews and Martinez.

"Another department failure," Andrews muttered, frustration evident in his tone. "How's it feel Sanchez? To lose for once."

"Not so good, but then again probably the only time I ever will," Sanchez jested.

"It's alright, we'll press on. We're used to it," Martinez joked back. "But we can't afford to stop now. We will get another chance soon enough."

Sanchez nodded and stepped out of the vehicle, watching the van disappear into the night. He walked alone, pride swelling in his chest from the support he had tried to provide. Despite the setbacks, he knew he had given his all and had been a valuable asset to the operation.

When he reached his car, he took a deep breath, savoring a small but significant sense of accomplishment. As he turned the key in the ignition, a faint smile crossed his lips. Suddenly, the night was shattered by an explosion, flames consuming the car in a fiery inferno.

***

Andrews and Martinez were just 15 minutes away when the explosion rocked the air, followed by a flood of emergency calls. Their hearts clenched as they realized it was near where they had left Sanchez. Andrews whipped the van around, flooring the gas pedal back to Sanchez's last known location.

When they arrived, the car was still engulfed in flames, fiery tendrils clawing at the night sky. Andrews tried to approach, but the searing heat forced him back. A crowd had already gathered at a safe distance, while the wail of sirens grew louder.

Andrews' face twisted in shock and horror. "Sanchez!" he shouted, but there was no response. Deep down, he knew it was too late.

Martinez, eyes wide with disbelief, edged closer. "We just left him... How could this happen?"

Guilt washed over Andrews like a cold wave. "Did we set him up to die?" he murmured.

Martinez shook his head, struggling to comprehend. "We couldn't have known. He was just supposed to meet Tao... It wasn't supposed to end like this."

Flames consumed both the vehicle and Sanchez's lifeless body. Andrews and Martinez stood by, watching as firefighters battled the blaze, gradually bringing the inferno under control. In the alley behind the burning vehicle, a tall man with a cigarette caught Andrews's attention. He smiled briefly before vanishing into the shadows. Andrews sprinted around the vehicle to the alley, but the man had disappeared.

They stayed until the fire was completely extinguished, leaving only a smoldering wreck. The untimely death of their team member, Sanchez, underscored the peril they faced. In this line of work, no one was immune to the reach of death.

***

Harper seamlessly blended into the energetic ambiance of the club, becoming one with the exuberant and animated crowd. The rhythmic melodies reverberated from the speakers, creating an intense volume that seemed to lift patrons off their feet. His eyes methodically swept the room, searching for Isabella Vargas. Her image remained fresh in his mind, obtained by infiltrating the city's databases.

He spotted Vargas in a VIP booth with Jin Tao, flanked by bodyguards. Their tense body language hinted at internal discord and concealed information. Unlocking his phone, Harper navigated to the app he designed, scanning nearby devices. They populated on his screen, ready to intercept communications. He attempted to connect to Jin Tao's phone but failed, so he tried Isabella Vargas's phone and succeeded.

The conversation started mundanely—business dealings and updates on Nightshade operations.

"We need to shift our strategy now," Vargas said, her voice low and sharp. "Our friend has worked as planned, just as Mr. S said. Cartwright and Delgado's operations have been turned over to you. And my cut, well… it's been more than generous."

Jin Tao nodded. "Yes, we need to take this Harper out of the picture now that he has fulfilled his purpose." His phone vibrated, and he typed a message back.

Harper's head started throbbing, interrupting his revelation of being used as a puppet. His breathing grew shallow as he attempted to walk away, the pain slowing his steps.

His legs buckled, forcing him to brace himself against the wall. The earpiece he used for tactical listening began to emit static. His phone's screen flickered erratically, an unmistakable sign of a counter-hack.

The thumping beats of the club music intensified, drowning out all other sounds. He stumbled to the ground, his hands drenched in spilled drinks. Looking up, he saw Jin Tao and Isabella Vargas across the room, their piercing gazes locked on him. They had found him.

Heart pounding, Harper summoned all his strength in a desperate attempt to escape. Suddenly, a firm grip seized his arm and shoulder, propelling him onto a nearby table, shattering glasses and spilling drinks. The club music halted abruptly, turning dancers into shocked spectators. Harper winced in excruciating pain on the floor, as another hand grasped his injured shoulder and flung him into the crowd. Struggling to regain his composure with the aid of nearby hands, Harper rose to his feet. The attacker advanced, reaching into his coat to reveal a hidden firearm.

In an instant, Harper grabbed a nearby bottle and hurled it toward the man's face. The glass shattered into a hundred shards, piercing his eyes. Blood seeped from the wounds like crimson ink from a broken pen. Harper took advantage of the moment, shoving the man into the crowd to create distance as he maneuvered through the throng of bystanders.

As he made his getaway, a voice shouted, "Gun!" causing the club to erupt into chaos. Harper glanced back to see patrons trying to restrain the gunman while others fled in panic, screams filling the air. Drinks splattered across the floor, the pungent smell of alcohol mixing with sweat and fear. Harper dashed for the exit, adrenaline fueling his every step. As he reached the door, he locked eyes with Vargas, who watched him with a malevolent smile, her gaze icy and conniving.

He scurried through the crowd, evading his pursuers. Harper was no longer in the shadows, and Isabella Vargas knew it.

***

Andrews was deep in thought, reviewing reports on his computer with Sanchez's death fresh on his mind. The leaders of Nightshade had met a grim fate, leaving Isabella Vargas as their sole survivor.

"I appreciate you all being here today," he began, addressing his team. "I know the death of Thomas Sanchez weighs heavily on our hearts. He died trying to bring down the WDT. But he wouldn't want us mourning, not just yet.

Andrews addressed his team, his tone resolute. "We need to focus on the task at hand. Hector Cartwright and Carlos Delgado have both been assassinated in the last couple of days. While this might seem like a good thing, WDT activity is rising. We still lack evidence to link them to the murders. Frank and Donovan, I need you both to monitor Vargas. If there's a connection between our mystery subject and the assassinations of Nightshade's leadership, it's only a matter of time until they target her next."

Captain Reed stepped out of his office, his face grim, worry lines etched deep into his features. "Andrews, my office, now!"

Andrews stood up, weaving through the maze of desks toward Reed's office. The captain stood by the window, staring out at the department's parking lot, the afternoon light reflecting off Reed's army medals. His posture was rigid, his demeanor one of stern authority, a clear reflection of his disciplined military past.

"Andrews, how long have you been working the triple homicide?"

"It's been a little over two weeks now, Captain, but Berg and I are making progress—"

"Stop," Reed snapped, his eyes narrowing as he turned to face Andrews. "Two weeks, and you haven't brought in any suspects? Instead, you keep piling up more cases, more murders, and you have nothing to show for it?"

"Sir, we are close, I just know it. I've set up a team to monitor Isabella Vargas, one of the Nightshade leaders."

"Monitor her, for what? Do you really believe your team can stop the killer? Think about it. Two of Nightshade's top figures are dead. Who could infiltrate their networks so effectively while we're left in the dark? One was locked in a warehouse by some hacker and killed. The other's vehicle was hacked and driven off a cliff. The consistent link is the murderer's advanced tech skills. That can't be a coincidence, don't you think?"

Andrews took a deep breath, acknowledging the truth in Reed's words. "You're right, Captain. The technology angle is our strongest lead, and Berg is working on it. I'll reexamine the evidence and see if there's any common thread we missed."

Reed's expression hardened, his voice sharp as a command. "Good. And let me be clear, Andrews. If you don't bring me any updates in the next two days, you'll be looking at a demotion. Understand? I need results, not more dead ends."

Andrews met Reed's unyielding gaze, determination steeling his voice. "Understood, Captain. I'll get on it right away and ensure we have solid progress within two days."

Reed nodded, his tone slightly less harsh. "Alright, then. Now get back to work."

Andrews returned to his desk, reflecting on Reed's words. He was right; technology had been the consistent link in these murders. As he stared at the cluttered bulletin board, his eyes were drawn to a photo of Nightshade's emblem—the eclipse tattoo. The image triggered a memory, pulling him back to his conversation with Harper at the hospital. Harper had been a wreck, his voice barely more than a whisper as he spoke.

"I'm just a cybersecurity analyst," Harper had said, his voice strained with grief. "I help the government with ethical hacking."

The memory lingered, and Harper's expertise in cybersecurity seemed like a significant piece of the puzzle. He had mentioned finding security flaws, simulating attacks, identifying weaknesses—all skills that could prove useful in these tech-driven murders.

Andrews rifled through his files, searching for Harper's records. He grabbed Harper's photo and employment history, then rushed back to Reed's office, his heart pounding with the excitement of a breakthrough.

"James Harper," Andrews said, showing the captain a photo.

"What about him?" Captain Reed adjusted his reading glasses to scrutinize the image.

"Sir, it all connects. Harper's family was murdered, and he identified one of the intruders by the same eclipse tattoo. I think he may be our Suspect X. He's got a personal vendetta against Nightshade. Cartwright and Delgado were killed using advanced technology and hacking skills, which Harper possesses. Here's his employment record—he was a lead developer and hacker for the Department of Defense."

Reed studied the file. "If Harper's our guy, then this is more than just a revenge mission. He's dismantling Nightshade piece by piece. We need to move fast before he strikes again."

Andrews nodded, determination hardening his resolve. "I'll coordinate with the surveillance team. We can't afford to lose him now."

Reed's voice turned steely. "Then what are you waiting for, Detective? Go bring him in."

Andrews grabbed his coat and hurried out, a sense of urgency propelling him forward.

***

Harper realized his safety was compromised. Vargas had identified him, and he knew it was only a matter of time before she closed in. He rushed back to his hotel room, hastily transferring critical files onto a USB drive. With a few keystrokes, he activated protocols to erase all data from his systems, watching intently as files disappeared and servers wiped clean.

He threw several days' worth of clothing into a bag and secured his handgun. As he stepped into the hallway, he saw Detective Andrews emerge from the elevator with a patrolman. "Harper!" Andrews shouted, his voice cutting through the air. "Don't move!"

Panic surged through Harper. He spun around and sprinted toward the service stairs at the corridor's end. The sound of Andrews and the patrolman's footsteps grew louder behind him.

Harper slipped into the stairwell just as Andrews rounded the corner. Moving swiftly, he descended the stairs, his heart pounding in his chest. Halfway down, he heard the door slam open above him. Andrews was hot on his trail. Harper skipped steps, his hand skimming the railing for balance.

On the second-floor landing, Harper glanced back. Andrews was just a few steps behind, his eyes locked onto Harper. Harper pushed off the railing, bolting down the next flight. He burst through the door to the second floor, sprinting down the hallway. Andrews was right behind him, closing the gap with every stride.

Harper reached the far end of the hallway and darted into another stairwell. He flew down the steps, hearing Andrews' footsteps echoing close behind. Just as Harper reached the ground floor, he spotted an exit sign and bolted toward it. He shoved the door open and stumbled into the blinding sunlight of the alley.

Breathing hard, Harper dashed toward the street. He glanced over his shoulder and saw Andrews bursting through the door, only a few feet behind. Harper pushed himself harder, rounding the corner and nearly colliding with a hotel employee.

"Hey, watch it!" the employee shouted, stepping into Andrews' path. The brief obstacle gave Harper a crucial second. Andrews sidestepped the employee, frustration etched on his face, but the delay allowed Harper to gain some distance.

Harper sprinted through the alley, ducking behind a large dumpster as a patrol car cruised by. The officer inside scanned the area but didn't spot him. Harper held his breath, his pulse racing. The patrol car moved on, and Harper slipped out from behind the dumpster, heading for the bus stop.

As he reached the stop, a bus pulled up, its doors hissing open. Harper boarded, casting a quick glance back. Andrews was at the alley's mouth, having just cleared the obstacle course of hotel staff and patrons. Their eyes met for a fleeting moment, frustration and determination mirrored in both.

The bus rolled away, and through the window, Harper saw additional officers swarming the building. He had bought himself precious time.

Back in Harper's hotel room, "Berg, get in here," Andrews called. She entered, quickly assessing the scene. "Search these systems for any evidence Harper may have left behind," he instructed.

Berg immediately set to work, connecting her laptop to Harper's equipment. Her fingers danced over the keyboard as she began to unravel the traces of Harper's digital footprint, hoping to find the crucial lead that would point them to his next move.

While Berg got to work, Andrews quickly called the tech team to track Harper's credit card usage and directed another team to maintain surveillance around the hotel room. Every second counted, and he was determined to find Harper before it was too late.

Outside, Isabella Vargas watched the police enter the hotel, then instructed her driver to move on. She quickly called her men, offering a generous reward for Harper's immediate capture. She was determined to find him before the authorities did.

***

Hours later, Andrews sat at home, sipping whiskey. The warm liquid offered a brief respite from the day's stress. The quiet of the evening was broken by the sudden ring of his phone. Andrews glanced at the screen and saw Berg's name flash across it.

"Andrews, I found something," Berg said without preamble when he answered.

Andrews straightened in his chair, immediately focused. "What is it?"

"Harper's credit card was tracked at several locations including a gun shop and Foundry Tech a few days after the murders. Credit card logs show: a 9mm pistol, a laptop, surveillance equipment, and several other technology devices. I also checked in with his employer and coworkers—they said he hasn't shown up for work in weeks except for one time to retrieve some notes."

A surge of adrenaline coursed through Andrews. "Berg, what would we do without you? This is exactly what we needed. I'll coordinate with the boss to put out an alert to all patrols."

He hung up, his mind whirling with the new information. Harper was a man on the run, but now they had a tangible trail to follow. He quickly dialed Captain Reed, waiting as the phone rang.

"Andrews, this better be important," Reed said, his tone tinged with irritation, the clinking of dishes audible in the background.

"Captain, we've got a lead on Harper. Berg found that he used his credit card at an electronic store days after the incident. He bought surveillance equipment and a VPN subscription. His employer and coworkers confirmed he hasn't been to work in weeks."

Reed's tone sharpened with interest. "That's solid. What's your plan?"

"I think we should set up a surveillance operation around the tech store and monitor his credit card activity closely. We need to move fast, Captain. Harper is clever and won't stay in one place for long."

"Agreed. I'll mobilize additional resources and get some plainclothes officers on the ground."

"Thanks, Captain. I'll coordinate with the team and make sure we're ready for any developments," Andrews said.

"Good work, Andrews. Send out a Be on the Lookout (BOLO) message disseminated to all agencies for a James Harper. Let's bring him in."

Andrews ended the call and immediately started organizing the operation. He instructed his team to prepare for a potential encounter and ensured that all necessary measures were in place.

With every detail falling into place, Andrews knew the next few days would be crucial. Harper was clever and resourceful, but they now had a lead. The stakes were higher than ever, and Harper had eluded them long enough. This time, Andrews was determined not to let him slip through their fingers.

He took one last sip of whiskey, setting the glass down with finality. The hunt was on, and he was ready.

CHAPTER 17: ISABELLA VARGAS

Isabella Vargas paced in her opulent office, cigarette in hand, her frustration unmistakable. Dark wood paneling, expensive artwork, and luxurious furnishings surrounded her, emphasizing her extravagant taste.

"Why haven't we found him yet?" Her tone was sharp and frosty, breaking the silence like a blade.

Marco, a brawny man with scars from countless battles fought on her behalf, stood casually before her. "We've got our men stationed throughout the city. We're also scouring surveillance footage. Harper won't evade us for long."

Vargas moved towards Marco, her steps slow and deliberate, closing the distance with an almost seductive grace. She stopped inches from his face, locking eyes with a cold, calculating intensity before exhaling a cloud of smoke into his face.

Turning away, Vargas walked to the large map dominating the wall, marked with pins on the Industrial District, South Valley, and the Docks—her strongholds in Foundry Hills. A photo of Harper, obtained by hacking his employee records, was pinned to the wall. She leaned in and kissed it, leaving a red lipstick mark on his lips, a glaring red dot in a labyrinth of notes and photographs—a complex web converging on one man.

Turning back to Marco, she inquired, "Marco, what compels you to engage in such a perilous endeavor within this enterprise? What drives your actions?"

Marco shifted uncomfortably but maintained his composure. "Loyalty to you and the organization, madame. Plus, the rewards that come with it."

Vargas smiled, a predatory glint in her eyes. She walked closer, holding a knife. "Loyalty and rewards," she echoed thoughtfully, her voice dripping with mockery. "But loyalty is such a fragile thing, isn't it? Easily bought, easily lost."

Without warning, she pressed the knife to Marco's neck, her grip firm. Marco's eyes widened, a flicker of fear flashing across his face. He swallowed hard, his subtle terror evident to Vargas.

"And w-what about you, madame?" Marco asked, his voice trembling slightly. "What drives you?"

She laughed, a cold, harsh sound that filled the room. "Power, Marco. Absolute and undeniable power. I intend to solidify my hold now that Hector and Carlos are dead." She paused, her smile turning into a grimace. "And to rid this city of the White Dagger Triad."

She moved the knife from Marco's neck and hurled it across the room, the blade embedding itself in Jin Tao's photo on the map. "They're next. But first, we find Harper. He won't escape. Double the reward. Find me the man of Foundry Hills. I want him alive."

As Marco exited, Vargas reclined into her leather chair behind the imposing desk, her fingers tapping an impatient staccato on the polished wood. Her phone rang, and she answered slowly. "Mr. S," she said.

"Isabella, why isn't Harper dead yet?" Mr. S's voice was cold and cutting. "I'm not pleased with your progress. This needs to be resolved immediately."

Isabella's jaw tightened in frustration. "Ensure it happens or you will join your former associates where your luxurious life won't follow," Mr. S replied icily.

Her temper flared, and she didn't hold back. "Don't forget who you're talking to! Threaten me again, and you'll find yourself joining them first. Harper will be dealt with on my terms," she snapped, ending the call with a sharp tap.

Still fuming, she immediately dialed Marco. He answered on the second ring.

"Marco, I need you to find a top-tier tracker," she ordered.

"Understood, madame. Any specific target?" Marco asked, sensing the urgency in her tone.

"Yes. I want you to track down a 'Mr. S.' I want to know everything about him," she replied coldly. "He thinks he can threaten me? I'll show him what real fear is. Hunt him down! I'll make him regret ever crossing me." Marco hesitated for a moment but he knew better than to question her. "I'll get right on it."

Isabella hung up, a sinister smile curling her lips. She leaned back in her chair, inhaling deeply from her cigarette before exhaling slowly, savoring the control she wielded. No one would threaten her position or her power. Not even Mr. S.

Her phone rang again; it was one of her lieutenants. "What is it?"

"We've spotted Harper near the docks," the lieutenant reported.

"Good. Keep eyes on him but do not engage. I want to know his every move," she instructed.

"Understood, madame."

Isabella ended the call and allowed herself a moment of satisfaction. Harper was just one piece of the puzzle. Mr. S would learn the hard way that no one crossed Isabella Vargas and lived to tell the tale.

***

Harper returned to the hotel where his room was previously raided by police. He waited in the lobby for Margaret, who routinely passed by after her workouts. Like clockwork, she entered the lobby.

"Margaret."

"Harper, are you okay? I saw the police in your room the other day."

"It's fine. I need you to hold onto something for me."

"Sure, what is it?"

"Here, please hold onto it. If anything bad ever happens to me, I want you to give this to a detective named Shawn Andrews."

"Of course. Are you in some sort of trouble?" She said, looking at the USB in her hand.

Harper nodded. "It's best if I don't tell you. But please promise you will give it to him."

"I promise."

"Thank you. Goodbye, Margaret."

She returned the gesture, and they both parted their separate ways.

Later that morning, the market near the docks was crowded, and Harper kept his movements fluid yet cautious, blending seamlessly among the sea of people. The vibrant colors and sounds of vendors shouting their wares created a chaotic backdrop. While examining a stack of apples, he noticed a burly figure lurking nearby, someone he recognized as one of Vargas's men.

Feigning nonchalance, Harper picked up an apple and deliberately dropped it, causing it to roll away. He then darted between stalls, knocking over a display of oranges in his haste. The vendor shouted angrily, drawing more attention. The burly man, realizing he had been spotted, abandoned his subtle approach and pushed through the crowd with purpose.

Harper zigzagged through the market, using the thick crowd as cover. The muscular man was relentless, shoving people aside as he closed in. Harper's breath came in short, sharp gasps as he spotted a narrow gap between two seafood stands. He squeezed through, emerging near a row of docked fishing boats. The smell of saltwater and fish filled the air as he ran along the pier, his shoes thudding against the wooden planks.

He glanced back and saw the man sprinting at him, closing the distance. Desperation fueled his sprint. Emerging onto a quieter section of the docks, he stumbled, frantically considering his options. Ahead, he noticed a small boat with its engine idling, the captain busy unloading crates of fish.

Harper dashed towards the boat, leaping onboard just as the captain turned in surprise. "Hey, what are you doing?" the captain yelled. Harper quickly gestured for the captain to be quiet, his expression pleading for cooperation, then ducked below deck to hide. Moments later, the muscular man arrived at the edge of the dock, scanning the area.

"Did you see a guy run by here?" the man demanded in a harsh tone.

The captain, looking annoyed, shook his head. "No, haven't seen anyone."

"Are you blind, old man?" the muscular man sneered. "He couldn't have gotten far."

The captain stood his ground, his expression stern. "I told you, I haven't seen anyone. Now get off my boat."

The muscular man cursed under his breath and moved on, continuing his search elsewhere. Harper let out a slow breath, a wave of relief washing over him. He knew he had only bought himself a little time. He peered out from his hiding spot cautiously and saw that the coast was clear. Clutching his throbbing ankle, he limped back onto the dock. Each step was agony, but he pushed on, weaving between the boats and crates.

He finally found refuge near one of the boathouses, collapsing behind a stack of nets and barrels. Harper clutched his ankle, knowing it was likely broken. The adrenaline was wearing off, replaced by searing pain that made him wince with every movement.

Minutes later, the sound of heavy footsteps approached. Harper's heart pounded as the boathouse door creaked open. The muscular man from before stepped inside, a smirk spreading across his face when he spotted Harper.

"Thought you could get away, huh?" the man chuckled, moving closer. Harper tried to scramble to his feet, but the pain in his ankle was too intense.

As the muscular man grabbed Harper, adrenaline surged through Harper's veins despite the searing pain in his ankle. With a firm grip, the man dragged Harper away from the boat, navigating through the maze of dockside clutter—crates of fish, coils of rope, and stacks of equipment. Harper stumbled along, each step sending sharp jolts of pain up his leg. The man's rough handling added to his discomfort, his fingers digging into Harper's arm like vices.

They emerged onto the cracked pavement of the dockside road, where a few parked cars lined the curb. The harsh midday sun beat down on him. Harper's heart pounded as he realized his precarious situation—the man's grip tightening, the approaching patrol officers, and his lack of options.

Just as they reached the edge of the sidewalk, two uniformed officers spotted them. Their patrol car was parked nearby, the red and blue lights reflecting off the dull metal of the vehicle. One of the officers, a seasoned veteran with a no-nonsense demeanor, called out sharply, "Hold it right there! What's going on?"

The muscular man, caught off guard but quick to react, released Harper and raised his hands slightly in a gesture of innocence. "Nothing, officer. Just helping my friend here to our vehicle."

The officers approached cautiously, eyeing Harper, who stood slightly behind the man, his hands slightly raised as a sign of surrender. The officer closest to Harper glanced at him and then at his partner, exchanging a quick nod.

"Sir, step away from this man," the officer commanded, his tone firm. The muscular man complied, stepping back slowly with a self-assured grin, as if he had nothing to hide.

The officer turned his attention to Harper, assessing him with a practiced gaze. "What's your name, son?"

Harper did not respond.

The second officer stepped closer, pulling out a document from his utility belt. He showed it briefly to his partner, who nodded again before looking back at Harper.

"James Harper, you are under arrest for the murders of Hector Cartwright and Carlos Delgado," the officer announced formally, reaching for his handcuffs. "You have the right to remain silent. Anything you say can and will be used against you in a court of law."

Harper's heart sank as the cuffs clicked into place around his wrists. He glanced briefly at the muscular man, who now stood a few feet away, his expression unreadable. The reality of his capture settled in—a bitter mixture of relief that the chase was over and fear of what lay ahead.

The officers escorted Harper to their patrol car, guiding him into the back seat with practiced efficiency. As they drove away from the docks, Harper sat in silence, staring out the window, finding it hard to believe that after everything he went through, this was the way it would end.

***

Harper sat hunched on the cold metal bench in his cell, staring out the barred window. Moonlight painted long shadows across the concrete floor. The echo of footsteps punctuated the silence of the police station. Remorse consumed Harper; Hector and Carlos, high-ranking figures in Nightshade, had paid for their actions, yet Isabella, the final piece in his vendetta, remained elusive.

The clang of the cell door opening startled him. He looked up to see a woman standing there, her blue eyes behind gold-trimmed glasses. She stepped inside, the door clanging shut behind her, and approached Harper with quick, purposeful strides.

"Who are you?" Harper asked, his voice hoarse from disuse.

She glanced over her shoulder, ensuring they were alone. "I know who you are, Harper. I know what you've done," she said, her voice low but intense. "You're the tech genius who's been unraveling Nightshade's organization."

Harper's eyes widened. "I am... but it was in vain."

"It wasn't. I'm Emily Berg, an analyst in the Police Department. I've been watching you, tracking your moves," she replied, her eyes never leaving his. "I know you killed Hector and Carlos. Isabella is the last one, and you need to finish this."

"Why are you helping me?" Harper asked, suspicion creeping into his voice.

Berg took a steadying breath. "My brother... he was a victim of Nightshade. He worked for Isabella Vargas as one of her bodyguards. It's true what they say about Nightshade; once you go in, you won't come back out alive—not by choice. She killed him," she explained, her voice tinged with sorrow and determination. "When I saw what you were doing, I knew there must be something I could do to help. Not just for you and what it stands for, but for my brother."

Harper nodded slowly, understanding dawning on him. "But Detective Andrews... if he finds out you helped me—"

"He won't," Berg interrupted. "I've planned this carefully. He's tied up with another case right now, and I've made sure the security cameras in this wing are on a loop. Come on, we only have a small window of opportunity."

Berg pulled out a set of keys and unlocked Harper's cell. "We need to move quickly. Follow me."

Harper raised himself off the bench, his muscles stiff from the cold. He followed Berg, limping through the narrow corridors of the police station. Berg moved with confidence, showing familiarity with every step. Harper felt a flicker of hope.

They reached a side exit, Berg pausing to check the hallway. "Okay, this way," she whispered, pushing open the door. The fresh night air hit Harper's face, invigorating him as they slipped out into the alley.

A gray car was parked nearby. "Get in," Berg urged, glancing around nervously.

Harper slid into the back seat, ducking low to stay out of sight. Berg quickly got into the driver's seat, started the engine, and maneuvered the car out of the alley. As the police station shrank into the distance, Harper glanced back, relief washing over him. "Thank you," he said, his voice filled with gratitude.

Berg kept her eyes on the road, glancing back at the rearview mirror. "Don't thank me yet. Save that for when we get you back to your place at the docks."

"How did you know?"

She glanced at him through the rearview mirror. "Because, like I said, I've been tracking your movements."

Harper nodded. "What am I going to do? Everything was taken from me at the police station—the gun, money."

"That's right. Here, I retrieved your items from the evidence officer," she said, handing him his bag.

"How were you able to manage this?" He started to change clothes in the car, storing the inmate outfit inside the bag.

"Pretty easy, especially when you're dealing with corrupt cops. To the department, this will look like it never happened."

"Thank you, Emily. I can't express how much this means to me."

"Don't worry about it. You need all the support you can get to finish what you started, with Isabella. I'm just glad I can help."

Harper grabbed his phone, turning it on. Thirty percent battery life and it still worked. At the bottom of the bag, staring back at him, was the glistening pistol, separated from the ammunition. He grabbed them both, reintroducing them.

As they approached the docks, his hideout came into view. Berg parked the car and turned to Harper. "Harper, I'm sorry for what you went through. I hope this is where you wanted to be in the end."

He looked out at the dark waters and the old, weathered buildings surrounding them. "Thank you, Emily. Me too."

Opening the car door, Harper stepped out, pain shooting through his leg, but his focus was on the gun gripped inside his hoodie pocket. He limped towards his hideout, tossing the clothes into a dumpster. The sound of the waves crashing against the docks echoed in the night. As he reached the door, he turned back to see Berg still watching him.

For a moment, he stood there, taking in the silence and the cool breeze from the water. The path ahead was fraught with danger, but he was more determined than ever to see it through. With a deep breath, he stepped inside his hideout, ready to face whatever came next.

***

The sounds of clacking heels vibrated through the container as Vargas paced furiously. A burly man sat before her on a chair, his hands bound in rope and his face covered by a dark hood. A lightbulb swung from the ceiling overhead, casting shadows that hovered like apparitions around the confined space. A boat's engine hummed in the background, a note of caution that it would be departing soon.

Footsteps alerted the man in the chair of a heavy-set individual approaching him. Yanking the hood, Marco revealed the man's fearful expression. His eyes darted around the container, trying to understand his fate, hoping someone would speak on his behalf.

"I gave you one simple order," Vargas hissed, her eyes burning with rage. She took a deep drag of her cigarette, exhaling as her eyes burrowed into the man. "Do not engage. Observe and report." Silence followed.

"But boss, the Harper guy, he saw me," he stammered. "I had to stop him to keep him from escaping. And there were police officers there. I thought maybe I could hold him for you."

"You thought? Maybe?" she interrupted coldly. "Marco, where do you get these idiots?" Marco shrugged.

"You were not supposed to think. You were supposed to follow orders. Observe and report back." She stepped closer, her face inches from his, exhaling smoke into his eyes. "And now, because of your incompetence, Harper knows we are onto him. Not only that, but we are back to square one."

The man swallowed hard, sweat dripping from his forehead, his subtle terror obvious to Vargas. "It won't happen again, I swear."

"You're right," she replied icily, drawing a polished gun from her coat, her gloved hand steady. "It won't."

Her face was cold and detached as she pulled the trigger, the bullet piercing his skull, the blood and brain matter following suit. The man fell backward from the chair onto the floor, motionless while the blood traveled on the ground.

Vargas watched him with disdain, then threw the gun onto his body. "Clean this up," she ordered Marco. "And find someone who can follow orders."

Marco nodded briskly, not daring to show any emotion. "Yes, madame."

Vargas turned away as the boat with the container departed the docks. She made her way to her car and drove away.

Outside her estate, she noticed a car parked nearby. Feeling suspicious, she parked behind them and grabbed a gun from her center compartment. The safety was off. With the gun in her left hand, she walked up to the car, approaching the driver's side window, smiling at the undercover officer. His eyes widened at the sight of her.

"What are you doing here, Detective?" she asked, her tone mocking.

"I'm here to ensure your safety. There is a potential threat following you," Andrews replied, his voice steady.

Vargas laughed harshly. "I don't need protection, Detective. Especially not from you. I can take care of myself. But you already know that, don't you?"

Andrews heard the click of a safety lever as Vargas turned on her heel and walked away. She laughed, waving at Andrews, her laugh still ringing in his ears, leaving him to ponder the enigmatic and dangerous woman he had just encountered.

Vargas poured herself a glass of Château Margaux. She slipped off her stilettos with a practiced motion and sank into a plush, velvet chaise lounge, its opulent fabric cool against her skin. She swirled the deep garnet liquid before putting it to her lips. Savoring the taste of the exquisite wine, she contemplated her next move. Her mind focused on where she was today—a crime lord at the pinnacle of her organization. No one would get in her way, not Hector, Carlos, Harper, Mr. S, or the police. She was not going anywhere, and she was going to make it known.

***

Harper's journey to the docks was a nerve-wracking ordeal, limping through every step. It wasn't merely a leisurely stroll through the city either. Since being chased by the burly man and the police, every movement was filled with trepidation and suspicion. His mind was a hurricane of doubts and fears coming at him from every direction.

He arrived at the docks, guided by the distant glow of streetlights. The air was gritty, tainted with oil—the essence of waterfront life. Enormous cargo ships drifted in the water, exchanging roles as full shipments arrived and empty ones departed. Their dark hulls reflected the faint, scattered lights across the docks. Containers were stacked high like colossal building blocks, concealing Vargas's clandestine activities from prying eyes.

Among the towering shipping containers, Harper desperately hoped Vargas would be at her estate, patiently waiting. Every passing minute stretched out like an eternity as Harper kept vigil over the barren landscape, his senses on high alert. Emerging from the shadows like a specter, a woman appeared, accompanied by her loyal enforcers. It was Isabella Vargas, without a doubt. Her silhouette loomed menacingly against the container backdrop as she guided her men.

Harper's heart raced as he observed Vargas exchanging words with her men. Tension mounted with every passing second. He observed as their mouths moved, unable to hear their conversation, but he didn't care. All he desired was to get closer, within arm's reach. He removed the clip from his gun, accounting for the 15 rounds that stood in wait. Harper pulled the slide back, loading a round into the chamber. His nerves were unsettling, causing his hands to shake. His fingers wrapped tightly around the pistol grip, ready for the opportunity.

Vargas's men moved towards another container. This was his chance. Harper advanced stealthily, cloaked in shadows. He was acutely attuned to every sound and movement, filtering out the backdrop of lapping waves and creaking ships, intensifying the atmosphere of tension and anticipation.

Entering an empty container, Harper felt the stifling air press against him with suffocating heat and clinging moisture. He pressed his ear against the cool metal, straining to hear the muffled voices from within. His pulse quickened as he caught snippets of conversation—the harsh rasp of Vargas's voice, footsteps echoing against the corrugated walls. Harper moved stealthily, closing the distance as the voices got louder, his gun poised. This was the moment—the final act.

Behind a wall of cover, his vision began to blur, faces of his family materializing before him, as if they were urging him to stop. "Don't do this, Harp," Denise's voice echoed. Alice and James Jr.'s faces joined Denise's, their pleading voices and eyes haunting him. Harper's grip faltered, causing him to stumble, nearly dropping the weapon. Hallucinations intensified, voices and images swirling chaotically, the ground beneath him moving like he was aboard a ship in a torrential storm.

"No, not now," Harper muttered, shaking his head. "I have to finish this." With immense effort, he refocused, reestablishing a tight grip on the gun, his mind focused on Isabella. Slowly and silently, he stepped past the cavernous dock to the lit window within the estate. Harper looked inside, finding Vargas sitting behind a desk.

Vargas dabbed her cigarette in the ashtray while carrying on a conversation on her phone, monitoring the screen on her computer. Her eyes narrowed in surprise as she spotted Harper, the interruption halting her actions mid-sentence.

"Well, isn't this a surprise," Vargas remarked, her voice tinged with intrigue as she peered up from her laptop and phone. She closed the laptop and set the phone down, her eyes never leaving Harper. "Why, Mr. Harper, you've finally found me," she added, her tone a blend of curiosity and amusement.

Jaw clenched, Harper took a step forward, confronting the woman who was singularly responsible for his suffering. "Cut the act. We both know why I'm here."

Vargas's lips curled into a cold smile. "You know, you are a remarkable man. I could use someone like you in my organization," she said, crossing her legs slowly, her demeanor calm and composed.

"You can't be serious. I'd never work for you. How could you even ask that after what you did?" Harper lifted the gun, pointing it toward her, the barrel centered on Vargas's head. His hands shook slightly, but his resolve was steadfast.

"Mmm... it's a shame. You know, this whole vengeance mission you're on, it's not what you think it is," Vargas replied, unfazed by the gun pointed at her. "Me, I'm only the executioner. I wouldn't have dreamed of causing you or your family harm, but how could I resist such an offer, to have Nightshade all to myself. Wouldn't you like to know who hired me?" She rose from her chair and walked towards a large board filled with information.

"You lie. This was all you."

"Hmm, true. I could have called off the job, except I didn't. I hold Foundry Hills within the palm of my hands, so I'll tell you who sent me. A man who is just as obsessed as you are with this whole charade of technology—the owner of SynTech. Well, as of recently, I believe he is your boss over at TechUse, or was. It doesn't make much difference to me who he is now."

"SynTech..." Harper's grip on the gun faltered slightly as he processed the information. "Mr. Seraphin?"

"Ah, so you do know him. Yes, Mr. Seraphin. He called me two weeks ago, talking about how we have a mutual interest in the changing leadership within Nightshade. He told me about a man who had a family that was key to his vision. Mumbling on and on about artificial intelligence and cybersecurity—it bored me. But he said if I did what he asked, he would give me Nightshade. I didn't believe him at first until he sent the picture of you and your family atop a suitcase containing half a million dollars. It didn't take much for me to get Carlos and Hector on board. But alas, my desires with Mr. Seraphin conflict at the moment. Rest assured, I will make him pay for your loss."

"No... you will pay." Harper's grip tightened on the pistol, his eyes blazing with fury. "You murdered my family."

Vargas's confidence wavered slightly, the smile fading from her face. "You stubborn, desperate man. Look at you, can't even compose yourself as you hold on to nothing. Fine, you want to know what happened?" Her tone turned psychotic. "How your wife wept before I put a bullet in her head." She slowly approached Harper, pointing at her head, reenacting the scene. The smoke from her cigarette curled around her like a sinister wraith. "A weak and pathetic Carlos said to spare the brats. No, when I do a job, I do it to the end. I followed them into their room closet while they huddled like scared little lambs, crying. I pulled the trigger, twi—"

A gunshot silenced the room.

Vargas held a hand to her stomach, lifting it to reveal a bloody patch on her black blouse. "You... No..." She attempted to walk back to her desk, but another gunshot sounded, hitting her shoulder and pushing her towards the back wall. She turned around, one hand on her stomach and the other on her shoulder, groaning in pain.

Harper was an arm's length away when he pulled the trigger yet again. This time, the bullet traveled through the middle of her forehead. She was pushed back, her knees collapsing beneath her, dragging against the wall. The wall was painted with a portion of crimson.

Harper approached her motionless form, his breath ragged, a grim sense of satisfaction mingling with the bitter taste of his vengeance fulfilled. Victory brought no solace as the weight of his actions closed in around him. He fled the scene as distant sirens pierced the air, disappearing into the night.

CHAPTER 18: GIVING IN

Hours later, inside a room surrounded by walls that concealed his truths from the outside world, Harper stood in front of the kitchen table. He stared down at the gun that had sealed Vargas' fate, gunpowder residue covering the tip of what once was a brand-new pistol. His eyes shifted towards the phone, picking it up off the table. The weight of the phone filled his mind with thoughts regarding his next steps. Numbers appeared as he pressed on the screen, followed by a ringing from the earpiece. Someone picked up the line on the receiving end of the call.

"Hello?"

"Sam, I need to see you."

"Harper?"

"Yeah, it's me," Harper's voice was hoarse, betraying the strain of the past 24 hours.

"Where are you? Are you okay?"

Harper hesitated, feeling the enormity of what he was about to reveal pressing down on him, almost suffocating. "I'm at a hotel, but listen, I-I need to talk to you."

There was a pause, pregnant with unspoken questions and mounting concern, before Sam spoke again, his tone soft but insistent. "Of course. Where can we meet?"

Harper swallowed hard, his mind replaying the events that led him to this moment. "The Grandview Hotel. Meet me in the lobby tomorrow morning, 9:30."

"Of course, Harper. I'll be there," Sam replied, his voice steady and reassuring.

"Thanks, Sam." Harper ended the call, a sense of foreboding settling over him.

Stepping outside his room, Harper squinted, raising his hand to block the intensity of the sun beaming down on him. His eyes adjusted, and he looked down towards the sidewalk. His feet pressed with purpose towards a steel pole denoting a bus stop. He took a deep breath, waiting for what seemed like forever, ignoring the pain ever present throughout his body. The bus arrived, and the doors hissed open.

"Afternoon," the bus driver said.

Harper nodded, attempting to make what he thought was a smile, except he was done pretending, and his body knew it.

"Mister, the fare is $3 dollars, you gave me $20?"

"Keep it," Harper replied, already making his way to the empty seats at the back of the bus.

The doors hissed shut. The driver looked back at Harper through the mirror, noting the burdened, exhausted look in his eyes and the weary limp to his seat. The driver's gaze lingered for a moment before driving off towards the next stop.

Harper watched the city fly by him, the bus stopping where riders waited and arrived. He noticed the field of headstones, the destination that awaited him. Slowly, the bus came to a stop about a hundred feet from the cemetery. He stepped down off the bus.

He made his way to a bench across from the graves of James Jr., Alice, and Denise. "Seraphin," he said in a soft whisper, wondering why he had directed the killing of his family. His hands trembled as he removed his glasses, his eyes remaining fixed on the horizon, the sun approaching its slumber for the day. From his pocket, he retrieved the emerald pendant, holding it close to his heart and breathing in the fresh air. A sense of peace washed over him, thinking about the love that had once filled his life slowly coming back to him. In that solitary moment, surrounded by the silent guardians of the dead, Harper found himself longing for death's sweet embrace, a release from the pain and grief that had consumed him.

***

Andrews looked down at the corpse leaning against the wall. Isabella Vargas had been a ruthless leader, living just as she had died—both simply equal. "Harper," he whispered. Vargas' death marked the last of the Nightshade members who carried the eclipse tattoo and were suspected of killing Harper's family.

He wondered what Harper was doing now that he had finished what he started. There was nothing else he could do at the scene besides waiting for the paperwork that would pile on top of the other two Nightshade leader murders. Andrews glanced back at the scene; he needed to find Harper.

The drive back to the station was somber, the city lights casting fleeting shadows on his face as he navigated through the quiet streets. His mind churned with thoughts of the fallen Nightshade leaders and the gap in control their demise had created. Andrews parked the car and stepped out, appreciating the cold night without rain. He made his way inside to the open floor where his office sat and officers stood by awaiting their briefing. The once red-pinned intel map on the wall was now riddled with white pins, each representing locations where the White Dagger Triad was exerting control.

"Everyone, listen up," Andrews said.

"Nightshade's loss of power means there is now room for someone else to take over unless we stop it. The White Dagger Triad, WDT, led by Jin Tao, is seizing the recent murders as opportunities to expand their operations. Although they deny it, we know that the WDT has been behind the various crimes affecting the city. That stops now. We have patrols increasing their presence at various WDT locations, forcing them to either stay in and cease their activities or for us to catch them in the act. If we keep the pressure on them, they are bound to break. Any questions?"

The officers, both uniformed and plainclothes, exchanged glances but remained silent.

"Got it, nothing heard. Also, as a reminder, we still have an active BOLO for James Harper. Take some copies on your way out and keep your heads on a swivel."

Andrews' gaze drifted to the map as the room cleared. Spots on the map where Nightshade's influence had once held sway were now reduced to mere shadows of their former selves. All taken over by the WDT, threatening to plunge Foundry Hills into further turmoil.

Later that evening, in the solitude of his home, Andrews received a call. The voice on the other end was as chilling as it was familiar.

"Detective Andrews," the voice said.

"Jin Tao. What do you want?" Andrews replied, his grip tightening around the phone. "You doing us a favor and giving yourself up?"

Jin Tao's laugh was a soft, sinister whisper. "No, but I do have something else to give you, Detective... truth. The Nightshade Organization's fall is part of a scheme, and Harper was just a pawn."

Andrews' jaw clenched. "What do you mean?"

"You think Harper's family was killed randomly? Then you have a lot more work to do," Jin Tao continued, his tone almost conversational. "This was all a necessary purge. Do not fool yourself into thinking this is the end. This is merely the beginning of something much grander."

The line went dead, leaving Andrews with doubts. He sank into his chair, thinking. Jin Tao's words unraveled a web of deceit and manipulation that stretched far beyond what he had imagined.

***

Sam arrived at the Grandview Hotel the next day as scheduled, precisely at 9:30. The lobby was quiet, with only a few guests walking about. He scanned the immediate area for any sign of Harper. He wasn't there. Sam continuously checked his watch; the minutes ticked by, still no Harper. He grew increasingly anxious.

By 9:50, Sam decided to approach the front desk. A young woman with a nametag reading "Catherine" greeted him with a polite smile. "How can I help you, sir?"

"I'm looking for a guest you might have staying here. His name is James Harper. Can you tell me if he's checked in? A gentleman with glasses, blue eyes? He told me to meet him here at 9:30." Sam asked, trying to keep his tone calm and collected.

"I'm sorry, sir, but we cannot disclose any information about our guests," Catherine replied, her smile unwavering but her tone firm.

"Please, it is very important. I just need to ensure he is safe."

She glanced at him before turning back to the computer, tapping the keys. Sam waited, hoping she would offer some information. Catherine passed him a post-it note with the numbers "314" written on it.

"Thank you," he said. She responded with a nod.

Sam entered the elevator, making his way up to the third floor. He stood outside room 314 and knocked twice. Nothing. "Harper?" Sam called out, his voice echoing down the quiet hallway. He knocked again, louder this time. Still, there was no response. Growing more worried, Sam looked through his phone for the call he received from Harper. He found the number and dialed it, but it went straight to an unconfigured voicemail. "Harper, I'm here at the hotel. Call me when you get this," he said, leaving the message.

Sam's mind raced with questions and concerns. As he made his way back to the lobby, he couldn't shake the feeling that something was wrong.

***

Detective Andrews arrived at the TechUse parking lot hoping to find Ivan Seraphin. He had planned to ask Seraphin a couple of questions regarding James Harper, hoping to shed some light on where he might be. Before he could enter, he found the scene was far from ordinary.

Federal agents swarmed the building, their presence commanding and purposeful. Andrews spotted Ivan Seraphin in handcuffs, surrounded and escorted by agents. Some of them carried confiscated computers and files.

"What's going on?" Andrews demanded, flashing his badge to one of the agents.

"We're placing Ivan Seraphin under arrest."

Seraphin, calm amidst the chaos, met Andrews' gaze with a knowing smirk.

"For what? What happened?"

A federal agent in glasses stepped forward to respond. "Mr. Seraphin here is tied to the use and manipulation of illegal technological practices and conspiracy with criminal organizations. I'm sorry, Detective, but that's all I can provide you at this time."

"Thank you for the information, agent." They both nodded to each other. While Andrews would have liked to make the arrest himself, the fact that the agents acted now meant they had secured evidence that would ensure Ivan Seraphin faced justice.

Back at his desk, Andrews reviewed the recent murders and the escalating violence that was attracting attention from his team. He shuffled through reports, each one detailing the brutal rise of the White Dagger Triad. The connections were clear, the patterns unmistakable.

"They're taking over," Andrews muttered to himself, frustration and determination mixing in his voice. "The power void left by the murders—they're filling it."

His mind raced as he pieced together the events. The fall of the Cartwrights, Vargas, and Delgados had not been random. It was a calculated move, orchestrated by someone with a vision for total control.

As he stared at the map pinned to his wall, dotted with the locations of recent crimes, Andrews knew that bringing down the WDT would be his next battle. The city depended on it, and he would not rest until justice was served. Andrews took a deep breath. The fight was far from over, and he was ready to face whatever challenges lay ahead. The White Dagger Triad's reign of terror had to end, and Andrews would be the one to make sure it did.

The rain pelted against the window as he sipped his lukewarm coffee, the bitter taste a grim reminder of the harsh truths he sought to uncover in the city's darkest corners.

"Any new leads on James Harper?" Andrews asked, his voice heavy with the weight of unresolved mysteries.

Martinez shook his head, the expression on his face grim. "Nothing yet, Andrews. It's like he vanished into thin air."

With a heavy sigh, Andrews rose from his desk, the unanswered questions taunting him like a leaden cloak. "I'm heading out to the morgue, pursuing another potential WDT murder. Call me on my personal if anything comes up." Martinez nodded.

The city streets glistened with the sheen of rain, the neon lights casting a sickly glow upon the slick pavement. Wiper blades cleared the rain, gliding it off the windshield. The streets slushed as he drove towards the coroner's office, his mind wandering to the latest case— a young woman found murdered in a dark alley.

Arriving at the coroner's office, Andrews stepped into the dim hallway, the scent of antiseptic mingling with the musty aroma of decay. A leak in the ceiling caused random drips of water to fall, echoing off the tiled floor like a mournful dirge for the lost souls that passed through these halls.

The coroner met him with a nod, his face obscured by the shadows cast by the flickering fluorescent lights. "Detective Andrews, here for the alley case?" he asked, his voice a low rumble that seemed to reverberate through the empty corridors.

Andrews nodded, "Yeah, how have you been, Brandon?" His senses were on high alert as he followed him deeper into the bowels of the building.

"Good, makes me miss my old nursing days. Moving the COWs around through the hospital."

"COWs?"

"Yeah, computer on wheels."

"Ah, got it. Clever term," Andrews responded.

He put his hands in his pockets, exhaling a visible cloud of breath. They approached the examination room where two gurneys were occupied by covered figures. Brandon picked up the chart. "Here we have the alley case victim. She has a laceration across the neck, the main cause of death."

"Can I get the report on her?" Andrews flipped through the pages. "This seems pretty straightforward. I'll pass it along to Martinez."

"Of course. I'll just need you to fill out the release form. Don't worry about this part…" He trailed off, noticing Andrews' attention had shifted to the other gurney. "Something wrong, Detective?"

"No, sorry, I was just drawn towards that covered figure. What happened to them?"

Brandon gestured towards it with a somber nod. "Another John Doe. Found him on a bench at the cemetery. He didn't have anything to identify him with. Just a gun, some cash, and an emerald pendant inside a backpack. We've set them aside for you over there."

"The cemetery?" Andrews asked.

"Yeah… um, near the graves of that family from the murders last month."

A chill ran down Andrews' spine as he approached the covered body. Brandon's gaze turned distant, his brow furrowing in concentration as he tried to recall the details.

"Can't remember the name," Brandon muttered, his voice trailing off into the gloom. "But I remember the story, it was a family from the outskirts of town—a daughter, son, and wife… the husband though, he survived somehow, who knows where he's at now. You think this guy has some relation to them?"

As Andrews unzipped the cover, the pale face of the deceased came into view, illuminated by the harsh glare of the overhead lights. He knew the face. It was of a man he had been hunting from the start. Brandon's voice broke the silence, his tone heavy with solemnity. "Yeah, this guy's cause of death was a mystery at first.

Based on the cosmetics, you would think he died from blunt trauma to the head—you see these wounds up here. He's got a fractured ankle as well, must have been a pain to walk with a strong determination to get where he needed to be. Anyway, none of those were the cause of death. This man here died from a brain tumor. Must have been excruciating—the pain and headaches he must have endured. Not to mention the potential hallucinations or visions he may have had."

Andrews nodded grimly, the pieces of the puzzle falling into place with a sickening clarity. "Harper," he whispered. The tumor had been the unseen specter haunting his final days, driving him to the brink of madness before claiming his life.

With a heavy heart, Andrews turned away from the macabre scene, the echoes of Harper's torment lingering in the air like a haunting refrain. In the darkness of the coroner's office, amidst the relentless downpour outside, he grappled with the harsh realities of a world steeped in shadows and secrets, knowing that the journey towards truth would be fraught with peril at every turn.

As Andrews exited the coroner's office, the rain had eased to a steady drizzle, and he pulled his coat tighter around him. Back in his car, he could not stop thinking of James Harper, everything he endured while pushing through the pain. Although grim, he was glad Harper got the ending he deserved—no man should have to live through all that. It seemed like a poetic ending.

The next evening, Andrews glanced at his watch, 7:45. There was still time. He made his way to a community center, a modest building that had seen better days. The peeling paint and flickering fluorescent lights did little to welcome visitors, but for Andrews, it was a place where he could confront his demons without judgment.

Inside, a circle of chairs was arranged in a humble room, filled with others seeking solace and understanding. The sign on the wall read "Alcoholics Anonymous," an inspiration of hope for those battling the liquid's addiction. Andrews took a seat, the creak of the plastic chair grounding him in the present moment.

The meeting began with the usual introductions, each person sharing their name and their struggle. Andrews listened quietly, his mind wandering through the labyrinth of his thoughts. When it was his turn, he took a deep breath and spoke.

"Hi, my name is Shawn, and I'm an alcoholic," he began, the words feeling both foreign and freeing on his tongue. The room responded in unison, "Hi, Shawn."

He continued, his voice steady but laden with emotion. "I've been drinking for a while now. I kept making excuses, perhaps part of the reason why I kept to the bottle. Sometimes it was the job, other times was the financial stress. But I believe the deep root of all of it was from the loss of my father. See, he was also a police officer who had an untimely death in the line of duty. Depression was hard to shake off, but when I took that first sip, it seemed like the only way for me to cope."

The group nodded in understanding, the shared burden of their struggles creating a bond stronger than words. Andrews felt a small measure of relief, knowing he was not alone in his fight.

"But I'm here because I want to change," he said, his voice firming with resolve. "I want to find a way to deal with the pain, the guilt, without drowning it in alcohol. I want to be better, for myself, for those who count on me. Someone recently inspired me. This man lost everything. But when he did, he saw only one way out. The way he felt was right when there were other avenues he could have pursued. Was he wrong in his actions? No, because that is what he thought was right. Like me, right here, right now. I am not perfect, and what I am doing may not be right, so I am here to fix myself before it is too late."

The attendees applauded and the meeting continued, filled with stories of struggle and hope, each one a test of the human spirit's resilience. As the hour passed, Andrews felt a sense of peace washing over him.

After the meeting, Andrews lingered for a moment, chatting with a few others who shared their own journeys. There was comfort in their camaraderie, a reminder that he was not alone in his battle. As the room began to empty, a woman approached him, her steps tentative yet purposeful.

"Hi, Shawn, right?" she said.

"Yes, hello, Margaret," Andrews replied.

She nodded, extending her hand with a warm smile. "I couldn't help but overhear a bit of your story. Mind if I join you for a moment?"

Andrews shook her hand, appreciating the genuine kindness in her eyes. "Of course." Margaret's presence was calming, and Andrews felt a surprising sense of ease in her company.

"Do you believe in fate?" she asked.

"I'm not sure. I believe things happen for a reason, but not that the reasons were already planned, if that makes sense."

She nodded. "It makes sense. I have something I was told to give to you." She handed him a USB drive. "A man named James Harper gave this to me and told me to give it to you whenever he was in trouble. Earlier this evening, I heard on the news that he passed away and was the primary suspect in several murders. I was going to the police department after this meeting, but here you are."

Andrews took the drive, his expression serious. "Thank you. Do you know what's in it?"

"No idea."

Andrews thought that if it came from Harper, it probably had some value. "This could be the break we've been waiting for," he said. "Thank you, Margaret."

She nodded.

***

In the precinct, Andrews loaded up the USB on his computer. Several videos, images, and documents filled the folder. He started a video labeled "Start with me."

"Detective Andrews, as you may already know by now, my name is James Harper. I make this video as a confession for my crimes and apologize for any ripples I may have caused during my last days. In the videos, you will see the murders of Hector Cartwright and Carlos Delgado. I understand that the third-order effects of my vengeance have created another monster, the rise of the White Dagger Triad, which brings me to the purpose of the content in this drive. In the file labeled 'Cartwright,' you will see Jin Tao himself, which I hope is enough to bring him to justice. I am sorry for everything I have done, but I am not finished. I need to find Vargas; she is the final piece. Goodbye, Detective."

"It's evidence. Connections between Jin Tao and Seraphin, and a video... a video of Jin Tao killing Cartwright. It's all there."

After watching the videos himself, Andrews knew he had enough to go with. He coordinated a raid on Jin Tao's stronghold at Rolling Peaks.

The team moved swiftly and silently through the mist-shrouded peaks, their breaths visible in the cold night air. This was their chance to dismantle a significant part of the criminal network plaguing Foundry Hills.

They reached the mansion that served as Jin Tao's fortress. Andrews signaled his team, and they moved into position. The element of surprise was on their side. With a nod, they breached the entrance, moving through the darkened halls with practiced precision.

Jin Tao was in his study, his back to the door as he examined maps and plans for his next move. The sudden intrusion caught him off guard. He turned, his expression shifting from shock to anger as he saw Andrews and his team.

"Jin Tao, you're under arrest for the murder of Hector Cartwright and for your involvement in organized crime," Andrews declared, stepping forward with his weapon drawn.

Tao's eyes narrowed, but he knew he was outnumbered and outmaneuvered. He raised his hands slowly, a sneer forming on his lips. "You think you've won, Detective?" he said, his voice dripping with contempt.

"We have. Tell me, what did you do to Hector Cartwright that caused him to remain motionless while he burned alive? I think you called it Aconitum whitei?"

Jin Tao stared in disbelief, lowering his hands. "How did you know?"

"Our friend Harper left us a little gift, a video of you at Warehouse 17."

Jin Tao's face hardened. He knew there was no escape. With a deep breath, he pulled out his dagger, a symbol of his heritage and honor. "Detective Andrews, in my culture, there's no greater shame than being captured and treated like a common criminal," he said, his voice steady.

Before Andrews and the other officers could react, Jin Tao made his choice, guiding the blade toward the middle of his chest, slightly left, targeting his own heart. "Better to die with honor than live in disgrace," he whispered, plunging the dagger in. Jin Tao's aim was accurate and true.

With Jin Tao gone, Andrews couldn't shake the feeling that there was still a lot to do. The connections they had uncovered would undoubtedly lead to more arrests.

As he stood on the misty peak, watching the lights of the city below, Andrews felt a sense of grim satisfaction. Justice for the Harper family was finally within reach, and he was determined to see it through to the end.

***

In the sterile, high-security environment of the state penitentiary, Seraphin sat in the common area, picking at his prison lunch. The room was filled with long, bolted-down tables, and the air smelled of overcooked vegetables and unidentifiable meat, dished out in lukewarm portions. Seraphin poked at the mound of mashed potatoes, his mind briefly wandering to how Harper had managed to achieve so much with his tech skills.

Nearby, a guard's voice cut through the din. "Keep it moving. No lingering around. You know the rules."

Seraphin's attention was drawn to a hulking inmate making his way through the rows of tables, his hand suspiciously close to his side, hidden from view. The inmate's eyes were cold, his movements deliberate.

Without warning, the man closed the distance, pulling a makeshift shiv from under his sleeve. The sharpened metal flashed briefly before it plunged into Seraphin's side. Seraphin gasped, his breath catching in his throat as the blade pierced his flesh. The inmate leaned in, his voice a harsh whisper.

"Marco sends his regards, for Isabella Vargas. No one threatens Nightshade."

The blade twisted cruelly before being yanked out. Seraphin slumped forward, blood pouring from the wound, pooling on the table and dripping onto the cold, concrete floor. The crimson spread, inching toward the metal drains embedded in the cafeteria floor.

Guards rushed over, shoving through the crowd of prisoners. "Get back! Everyone back!" they shouted, forming a perimeter. One guard called for medical assistance, his voice urgent and sharp.

Seraphin's vision blurred, the edges darkening as his strength ebbed away. Medical personnel arrived quickly, a young woman checking his pulse and looking into his eyes.

"Pupils fixed and dilated," she said softly, her tone somber.

The noise of the prison receded into a distant echo. Seraphin's final thoughts flashed before him as the world went dark, and he took his last breath.

***

Andrews' gaze fixed on the granite stone before him, the name James Harper inscribed upon it. Unspoken words can linger in the mind, gnawing at the soul with regret. His lips parted, releasing words steeped in admiration and sorrow. "Harper... you did more than dismantle Nightshade's organization. You took down the White Dagger Triad and unmasked Ivan Seraphin, something no one else could have done."

The wind picked up, swirling leaves off the ground in a dance of autumn colors. Andrews watched the leaves, admiring their freedom from burdens, contrasting with the heavy cloak of Harper's monumental achievements that settled on him. He stepped closer to the tombstone, the cemetery's silence amplifying the weight of his words.

"You were more than a hero to the people of Foundry Hills. I tried to be there for you and help you, but you did more for me and this city than I or an entire department of officers could have ever done."

From his coat pocket, Andrews produced an unopened bottle of whiskey and held it up. "This was once my escape, my way to hide from my problems instead of facing them head-on. Now, it's just a memory of who I once was, a man burdened by his own demons, haunted by loss and the constant shadow of death." The bottle clinked as he placed it atop the stone. His hand returned to his pocket, retrieving a green pendant. "And this pendant... it was always a part of you, a symbol of the Harper family's legacy and the love that drove you. Now, it is where it belongs. Thank you, Harper. I hope that in the afterlife, you have found peace and are reunited with your beloved family."

Walking away from Harper's tomb, Andrews' eyes fell upon a grave in the distance. An older man stood next to it, shrouded in silence and solemnity, resembling a faint image of his father. Andrews' heart quickened at the sight, drawing him closer.

Andrews saw the man clearly before passing behind the large oak tree, but once on the other side, the man had vanished. A sudden, sharp pain pierced his head, making him wince in agony. He leaned heavily against the tree, fighting to regain his composure. When he finally looked up again, the man was nowhere to be seen.

The sun broke through the clouds, casting a gentle light over the cemetery. Andrews exhaled deeply, the pain in his head easing. He glanced back at Harper's grave one last time before turning away.

***

Explosions rocked the city that night as doors were kicked in and criminals were hauled out. The shadows that once cloaked Foundry Hills began to recede with each successful operation. Andrews and his team moved with efficient precision, targeting White Dagger Triad strongholds in the Industrial District, South Valley, and the Docks. Crime rates plummeted, spreading hope throughout the town.

Andrews, standing amidst the ruins of the Triad's empire, knew that none of this would have been possible without the indomitable spirit of the man of Foundry Hills. Harper's legacy lived on, like the blade of Athena, embodying justice and resolve, paving the way ahead.

Made in the USA
Coppell, TX
16 July 2024

34679765R00104